When Dreams Find Wings

Mranes's heart and imagination yearn for the sky and adventure. And a glorious airhorse to take her there.
What will she learn about herself and the life ahead of her, on one special night when magic and desire collide?

Caught in Distraction, When She Needs Peace

Goresi faces one last challenge with a mind and heart full of chatter and nonsense.
And no time left for practice and patience.
Will a visit to her own past help her discover the way?

Pure Joy, and Fierce Competition

Conflicts with other fledgling airhorse riders prove the biggest challenge for Tonn.
Can he learn to overcome difficulties and trust himself?

Escaping Her Own Past

A mysterious voice from Dyna's past haunts her mind and threatens her happiness.
Will asking for help set her free, or send her deeper into madness?

The Heartbreak of Acceptance

Watching her son Arch struggle in silence shatters Selene's own heart. Only trying to get others to help her fight for him hurts worse.
Can she convince the ones who matter most to accept the truth and help Arch?

Fantastic Side Trips:
Side Characters Take Center Stage

Published 2021 by Spiral Publishing, Ltd.
www.SpiralPublishing.net
St. Paul, Virginia

Book and cover design copyright © 2021 by Spiral Publishing, Ltd.

Cover art copyright © 2021 by artecke | depositphotos.com

ISBN-13: 978-1-63992-006-8
Large Print ISBN-13: 978-1-63992-007-5
Hardcover ISBN-13: 978-1-63992-000-6

Library of Congress Control Number: 2021946287

Additional copyright information for previously published material at the back of the book.

For Crystal
Who encourages my girly side

And that's one reason these stories bring the bling!

FANTASTIC SIDE TRIPS

SIDE CHARACTERS TAKE CENTER STAGE

KARI KILGORE

SPIRAL PUBLISHING, LTD.

CONTENTS

INTRODUCTION

A few years ago, I took a wonderful workshop focused on writing in series. My assumption going in was we'd be talking about how novels and possibly novellas worked as part of telling a much longer tale.

Maybe different ways to keep the storyline logical and fresh, all while making sure each individual book's arc makes sense in the longer story. You know, fairly reasonable ideas and expectations.

And without a clue of the kind of scale the workshop aimed for, and I mean that in the best way possible.

While we did talk about the big story arcs in a series, the great eye-opener for me was getting down to the short story level. The reading assigned beforehand—almost all short story collections—should have been my first clue.

Turns out the vast, unexplored landscape of a fictional world offers countless fascinating side trips and excursions. Entirely made-up fantasy worlds even more so. Endless questions and curiosities that simply don't make sense within the focus of a novel, or possibly several novels.

Things like wondering what that sassy side character was

like as a child. Or where a dented and scratched trophy kept on the mantle came from. Curiosity about how the heroine's parents met and fell in love—or what drove their bitter divorce—often turn into interesting stories of their own.

I've long had a habit of writing notes to myself when I have questions like that, not much different than what you're reading right now. Not as a narrative, but more like a diary entry. Satisfying my curiosity and exploring the world, but not telling a proper story.

What hadn't really occurred to me until that workshop is there's no reason on earth that I shouldn't tell *myself* proper stories as I dig into those intriguing questions. After all, the whole reason I was drawn to writing in the first place was to write the stories I want to read.

Then of course the next logical question in my ever-curious mind was what to do with those self-contained excursions into the worlds inside my head.

Trying to shoehorn them into the novels or novellas truly doesn't make sense. If those bits of information and emotion were meant to be part of the main storyline, they would have shown up there in the first place.

And I find that kind of detour in the middle of another story a bit jarring in most cases. A few of our true master writers can pull it off, sure. But in less experienced hands, it hits me about the same way any unexpected detour or meander does: an annoying wander away from where I want to go.

After the excellent short story collections we read to get ready for the series workshop, and of course the workshop itself, I finally understood how many of those question/answer/exploration stories can stand perfectly well on their own. Others perhaps work best as a lead-in to the main series, or as an in-between treat for readers.

Some of my favorites are the Happily Ever After After

stories romance writers sometimes share, where we catch up with the happy couple and see what they've gotten into since The End.

And I've been answering my own fictional "I wonder what *that's* all about?" or "What's that corner of this world *really* like?" questions with side stories ever since.

That's resulted in quite a few short stories, of course, and a novella or two. I fully expect to end up with a novel-length reply to my curiosity at some point, or maybe a whole side series or two.

I've recently approached side stories on purpose as well, with the intention of venturing deeper into the worlds inside my head simply to find out what's in there.

With my collection *Facing Down Extraordinary: A Series of Ordinary Heroes*, I set out to write short stories based on side characters in different series worlds of mine, each in some variety of heroic role. In that case, I picked folks I wanted to know more about and let them tell me their stories. They were happy to oblige, and I had a wonderful time going back in story-time with them.

Fantastic Side Trips: Side Characters Take Center Stage started a little differently, but I had every bit as much fun with the writing. I'd just finished writing *Demon in the Air*, the second novel in *Misfortune and Magic. Misfortune and Magic* sits firmly in the alternate world of epic fantasy with castles and mages and magic, of course, and a huge world and storyline I'm only beginning to explore.

It's likely several more novels are on the way, and I have no doubt the world will continue to delight and inspire me.

So I decided to write side trips this time. Excursions into this vast world and all the secrets and surprises it holds.

Each story has a character from the first two novels at its heart, but they took me on an adventure through the parts of their world they know best. And wonderful tour guides they turned out to be.

Wings of the Heart visits with an airhorse rider named Mranes: one of the rare and lucky few who get to travel the world in speed and style on colorful flying horses. I started from a couple of lines of her dialog in the novels, and the story gave me all kinds of wonderful hints for future tales.

The powerful Honored Mages provide much of the mystery in these stories, and promise many tales about their origins, their distant city of Dirgelan, and what they know from centuries of studying and practicing magic. For *Footprints Along the Path*, Mage Goresi took me to Dirgelan in the long-ago days before she earned her title, and the respect and responsibility that came with it.

Obviously when one has a world full of multi-colored airhorses, one must learn more about them as soon as possible. So *Trusting Their Magic* visits the airhorse city of Maestar and a group of young riders-in-training. Mranes makes an appearance, but this story belongs to Tonn, her future wingmate, and to their entirely sensible airhorses.

The desert city of Profant plays a vital role in both *A Knight Sets Out* and *Demon in the Air*, as Baroness Dyna Bacalan and her husband Baron Hildar draw everyone into their family struggle. For *Lines of Strength and Grace*, I ventured back to the early days of their marriage, with the normal and not-so-normal adjustments of such a big change. One of the delightful rewards of writing these kinds of stories is I discovered Casai, another huge city that will certainly play a role going forward.

The bad-luck-inducing hero of the first two novels and possibly the whole series is Lord (and apprentice) Arch Knight, so venturing into his background and persistent misfortune was a natural for a *Misfortune and Magic* collection. His parents Selene and Moabar not only reveal his younger days, but also an insight into their relationship and parenting challenges in *The Difficulties Ahead*.

For anyone who's ever used a mapping app or GPS, writing these stories felt a lot like watching the details of the map filling themselves in. Combine that with learning so much more about characters I thought I already knew well, and *Fantastic Side Trips* became one of my favorite writing experiences.

Thankfully the world of these stories and novels gives me room for plenty of return trips, which I'll be happy to share!

I hope you enjoy getting to know these characters and taking these short excursions as much as I enjoyed writing them. Each is only a glimpse into the larger *Misfortune and Magic* world. You'll find the doorway at www. KariKilgore.com/MisfortuneAndMagic.

You'll discover more fantasy of many kinds at www. KariKilgore.com/Fantasy.

You can also visit www.KariKilgore.com to learn more about me and find other short stories, along with novellas, novels, and more collections.

If you want to keep up with what I'm doing next, get free stories, read exclusive content not available anywhere else, and see adorable pet photos, check out The Confidential Adventure Club at www.ConfidentialAdventureClub.com. Hope to see you there!

And last but certainly not least, thank you for your support of me and my writing. It means the world to me and keeps me coming back to tell the next tale.

KARI KILGORE

Wings of the Heart

A MISFORTUNE AND MAGIC STORY

For everyone who dreams
and makes those dreams come true

WINGS OF THE HEART

THE WARM, green-blue water sparkled under the early morning sun in the distance, creating the impression of a million glittering jewels dancing with the tide.

A group of silvery sea-hunting birds wheeled against the deep blue sky. Their sharp cries pierced the repetition of the waves scrubbing along the shore and splashing against the rocks under Mranes Dalgryn's water-roughened hands.

She'd heard a thousand stories of how the ancestors built the long, narrow pier in her village of Gartria when they first arrived in the land of Genfrith many long years ago. Transporting the rich orange and vivid black stones from outcrops a day's journey inland, then adding the sharp lines of mortar made from the bright red sands all around her.

The stone walkway extended far into the water, branching out into smaller piers so twenty ships could anchor safely. Everything from flat, shallow local fishing boats to solid, round-bellied day-boats with bright, colorful sails, bringing merchants and visitors from all along the jagged coastline of the great continent of Hanferthen.

Once in a while, and not nearly as often as Mranes

would have liked, the great trader ships from across the vast, cold, and dangerous Nifendraw Sea arrived, anchoring at the farthest point from shore where the seabed plunged to depths unseen and dangerous. Unlike the cheery day-boats sitting high in the water—with sunshades in equally bright tones allowing the travelers to enjoy their days sheltering from the warm sun—the trader ships were darker.

Quieter.

More serious, somehow.

They arrived under a billowing arrangement of ominous gray sails, with broad decks made of dark green wood that held no cushions for conversation or napping. The traders were designed to carried enough cargo that their sturdy decks were riddled with hidden doors for loading and unloading.

Or so Mranes had heard. She'd never seen much of the mysterious cargo or stepped onto one of the traders for herself.

Usually diverted from their normal first calling port of Masnarech far to the north near the rocky Gorowan Mountains because of dreadful storms, the people on board the traders at first seemed as odd as their ships. Men and women of all shapes and sizes, as varied as the clothing they wore, or the fine silk fabrics they brought from distant lands.

Tall and slender like her father, short and curvy like her mother, and everything in between. With hair brown or black, blonde or gray, striking green or gorgeous deep orange. Skin ranging from so pale she wondered how they didn't roast in the high sun at sea, to much darker than her own warm brown, to every shade from intense blue to mossy green to vivid purple.

Some with magic that helped them guide their huge ships safely through icy waters and past fierce creatures that could drag them under the waves more surely than the worst storm. Others supposedly with magic to help convince both sellers and buyers to agree to terms most agreeable to the traders on their ships.

Despite all that, the waylaid traders were always friendly once they reached the red sand beaches of Gartria.

Thankful for the long pier and deep harbor that could hold their ships with more under water than above, rather than forcing them to detour far to the west and the vast, bustling city of Casai. Putting in at Gartria allowed them to unload enough onto wagons headed north to allow safer passage along a coast that grew steadily more shallow and rocky.

Generous with their coin, smiles, and the goods they carried.

Providing yet another reason why the ancestors' hard work building the unusually long pier truly created the solid foundation that made their village's livelihoods joined with the sea possible today.

At least that's what Mranes had been told every time she expressed dismay at having to repair that mortar yet again when this day of community labor rolled around.

Several children both older and younger than her worked along the pier: some kneeling or sitting on the surface, others in the water like she was. A few adults lingered in tiny boats toward the deepest point, in case anyone slipped or got into trouble.

That and watching to make sure the vital repairs were done right.

In her more frustrated moments, Mranes was sure every bit of *half* of her one-day-short-of-fourteen years had been spent on this very spot.

Legs in the warm, salty water, bare feet in the shifting sand.

Loose-woven tunic and short breeches designed to dry almost as soon as it got wet either floating on the water or fluttering in the summery, flower-scented breeze. Today a tan version several shades lighter than her skin, cut long enough for the height she'd added seemingly overnight.

Hands aching from trying to fill in the gaps she'd scraped clean hours ago. Moving quickly enough so the mortar had a chance to set before the tide rose high enough to splash all of her hard work away.

Just the right mix of the smooth red granules with water-resistant sap from the squat, brushy wybar trees that grew all along the coast, with the astringent stink cutting through the salt-water air.

Even at her most annoyed, Mranes had to admit how amazing it was that the resulting sticky goop had kept the pier sturdy and functioning for all those countless years.

She leaned down enough to rub her hands together in the warm water and rinse away the remnants of sap. Thank all the powers that be, the lowest parts of the pier that never quite dried out even during the lowest tides were made of huge slabs of stone. Buried where their rough edges wouldn't catch and tear at feet and wagon wheels alike.

So only the walkway along the top had stones small enough to need all this bothersome maintenance. Mranes knew from knuckle-scraping experience how hard the stones were, how difficult they must have been to shape.

But sometimes she still wondered why the ancestors hadn't figured out how to quarry smoother pieces all those years ago.

Probably so their children and grandchildren and great-great-greats would get stuck with this same chore year after year, all in the name of respecting history or building responsibility or something equally strange the adults kept telling them.

Standing back up to her full height, Mranes brushed irritably at her thick brown hair that seemed to escape no matter how tightly she bound it away from her face. She'd tried braided strings of fabric or seagrass, long strips of cloth, even tucking it into one of her father's broad straw hats. Everything short of the intricate braids and twists reserved for married women.

Even if she *did* braid it, Mranes was sure it would work itself free to dance and tease and tickle her cheeks and ears and eyes in the wind. Then attach itself to her sweaty skin in the intricate new twists and tangles it was taking on.

Her mother said the same thing had happened to her hair at the same age, leaving the straight locks of childhood behind. But Mranes doubted the unruly mop on top of her own head would ever resemble her mother's lovely mass of shining curls.

Then her heart soared into her throat at movement low on the eastern horizon, where the land rose toward the stony heights of the Gorowan Mountains.

Perhaps an airhorse arriving with news, or simply for a visit along the warm Wrynath Sea?

The riders came here sometimes, more often than the huge trader boats, and far more exciting. Through the air or on one of the day-boats from the distant city of Maestar, home to airhorses and riders alike.

Her father said the riders worked far harder than anyone who fished or sailed or almost any other vocation, and that's why they needed rest and recovery in the sun for themselves and their glorious airhorses.

Flying urgent messages and important people about, like the powerful Honored Mages who wielded magic as easily as Mranes breathed. Swooping into distant lands full of fierce fighting, using their own weapons and clever minds to bring about peace.

All while astride great winged beasts in every color of the rainbow.

She refused to *believe* the more outlandish tales about mages from either her older brother or other kids.

Of course they didn't give themselves gills so they could lurk under the water and steal children away, or transform solid boat bottoms into transparent holes to drown people.

But she never refused to *listen* to those tales, so she wouldn't be surprised in case they ever did hold true.

And no matter how hard her father said airhorse riders worked, or how often she saw their weariness and sometimes injuries with her own eyes, Mranes never stopped daydreaming of becoming a rider herself.

Leaving her home and family behind, along with the tradition of working as a fisher like her mother, or a weaver like her father. Or even a teacher or merchant or sailor or any of the more adventurous lives she could lead.

None of those paths compared to the freedom of taking to the sky and going where she willed. And having a spectacular airhorse of her own, perhaps with a coat of yellow or purple or pink, and smelling of sweet flowers or fresh, rainy air like they often did.

The idea had taken hold deeply enough to show up in her sleeping lifetime as well, with constant nightdreams of holding tight as her very own airhorse swooped and dove, dancing through the air as easily as fish through water.

Just then what her wandering mind thought was a distant airhorse against the sky drew itself up into a compact arrow and streaked toward the waves. Mranes realized she'd been watching a much closer seabird, letting her imagination carry her away as it so often did.

"Got your head among the clouds again, love?"

Mranes jumped even though she knew the voice as well as she knew her own.

She turned to see her father standing on her same side of the orange and black pier, up past his knees in the swirling water. He was dressed much like she was, except he wore a broad woven hat to protect his lighter skin from the sun.

All his clothing was sturdy and plain, as opposed to the artwork in tunics, gowns, table and bed covers, and even wall hangings he produced for trade. She was constantly amazed at the designs that took shape under his hands, as if he used paints and brushes rather than cotton and wool and silk and grasses.

Between his work and Mranes's mother and her fishing, they had no worries when it came to coin. Like nearly everyone in Gartria, they made certain their family had every chance to read and travel and learn as much as possible.

None of that excused Mranes or anyone else in the whole community from their turn at the irritating, never-ending work of maintaining the pier.

She ducked her head, embarrassed she hadn't even heard him walk out so close to her.

"Just watching the seabirds hunt, Father," she fibbed. "A couple of big ones out there today."

He shook his head, but his eyes sparkled, the same green as her own.

"I'll wager you were wishing they were airhorses instead. Your mother talks of seabirds with wings longer than I am tall, but none you could actually climb onto and fly yourself away."

Mranes reached into her square wooden box full of mixed mortar, tied to the pier so it floated beside her, trying to hide her grin at how well her father read her mind. She was surprised to find almost all the sticky red mixture used up.

She scooped out a handful anyway and set about looking for gaps in the stepping stones in front of her, running the fingers of her free hand across the smooth, nearly dried lines. The narrow, sparkling seams between the rocks were barely tacky now, in plenty of time to avoid damage when the incoming tide sent water splashing high.

"I've heard the hunting birds in the north could even carry someone as tall as *you* away," she said, hopeful she might end up so wonderfully tall herself. "They snatch up sheep and cattle, even the great hunting cats in the mountains if the tales hold true."

Her father laughed as he also traced the mortar lines, nodding as he went.

"You know as well as I do how rarely the tales hold true. Especially when they're told as gossip to frighten children much younger than you are now. You do a remarkably good job with a task you dislike so intensely."

Mranes hesitated in filling in a gap so small she couldn't see it except with her fingers, long enough that a glistening bit of mortar splatted right into the middle of one of the orange stones. Her father swiped it away before she could.

"It has to be done, I guess," she said, again rinsing her hands in the sea. "And done properly the first time is best. If I don't pay attention and make a lot of mistakes, I'll be right back out here doing my whole section over tomorrow after everyone else is finished."

Her father shrugged, the corners of his mouth turning down even as his eyes smiled.

"That's possible, I suppose. I had to watch over a few younger than me who botched the job when I was your age. Do you ever worry you'll end up having to do the same since you're so good at this? Or that someone will suggest you help build the new pier we're forever talking about, but never starting work on?"

Mranes snorted laughter before she could help herself.

"You mean the new pier we don't actually need, and that no one wants to spend years carving out the big stones for?

That's not one of the fears that haunts my waking or sleeping lives, no."

"I'm glad to hear it. That would be a tedious way indeed to spend your sleeping lifetime. You're finished here unless you want to wade out and help the others. Ready to head home?"

Mranes glanced back out at the rest of the young people, all still busy at work. She couldn't argue with her father's assessment of her efforts, but she still felt a bit guilty about leaving before anyone else did.

"Will they get upset if I go now, Father? I don't want to make anyone feel bad."

He shook his head and gathered up the chisels and brushes she'd used to clean and smooth out the mortar lines.

"The younger ones won't likely notice. And the older ones will know exactly why you enjoy extra time this evening. Your birthday is tomorrow, remember? Your fourteenth."

Mranes grinned as she picked up the mortar box and walked with him toward the edge of the water. A wide stretch of the beach lay exposed, the sand fading from dark, nearly blood red to a brighter shade as it slowly dried in the sun. The color line would shift much higher as the tide turned and came back in.

She expected a fine meal this evening in her honor, and gifts. Hopefully books with tales of faraway lands, or maybe one of her father's fine tunics made especially for her. She preferred those to gowns, much to her grandmother's disappointment.

"I don't think I've ever forgotten my birthday, not since I was old enough to understand what it was."

"What you don't yet know is this one is special. Tonight your mother and I will help you recall your sleeping lifetime in a different way than we have before."

Mranes shivered as the breeze cooled her legs, startling after so long in the warm water.

And not a little bit from the idea of having one of her sleeping lifetimes recalled.

Like every family who had the rare talent for working with the lives lived behind closed eyes—here in Gartria and precious few other places—normally children only had their dreams recalled when they soured into nightmares. Revisiting those dreams with someone to help them seek the meaning and the source so often helped them shift from terror into understanding.

Which of course led to a huge and ever-increasing number of whispered tales about what sorts of sleeping lifetimes *adults* recalled.

She doubted many of those tales held true, but as with so many things for her, the wondering never ceased.

"What sort of sleeping lifetime will we recall, Papa?"

He smiled, probably at the little girl name for him she hadn't used in years.

"We'll explain it all to you when the time comes. For now, we'll go home and feed your endlessly empty belly after your hard day of work. Then you, your mother, and I will all celebrate the joy of you having fourteen years."

As afternoon drew down toward evening, Mranes stepped out into her backyard, freshly bathed and dressed in the most wonderful birthday gift she'd ever received.

Their orange stone house—made from broken rocks too small for the pier, if the tales held true—wasn't overly large. Most of the homes in Gartria were similar, with more space for living outdoors than inside.

The yard was more of a garden, with a border made of

every fruiting bush and tree that could be brought from anywhere nearby. Leaves ranged from as small as her thumbnail to as long as her arm. Mostly glossy dark green, but some of pink and blue and yellow.

Right now the night air bloomed sweet with glowing purple phertecha flowers as big as her hand, hanging from decades-old vines covering a gathering shelter in the corner. The addition of roasting fowl on the firepit had Mranes's stomach paying attention even though she'd stuffed it full of fish and sea greens not long ago.

She walked barefoot along the sand pathway toward the shelter, enjoying the warmth of the grains between her toes much more than she had along the pier that morning. Much as she might not have wanted to admit it during her earlier grouchy day, wearing one of her father's most beautiful tunics made all the difference.

He'd made it out of a shimmering deep blue silk, an indigo nearly black in the evening light, with swirling patterns like the sea waves worked in copper and gold thread. He'd even added intricate knots along the sides that would let her adjust it as she grew taller and added womanly curves like her mother.

A matching skirt made long enough to brush the ground waited in her bedroom, because he'd also made her a pair of lovely breeches. Not unheard of for a girl, but unusual. That thoughtfulness left her heart full to bursting, especially when she caught sight of herself in a mirror on the way out.

She recognized her face and eyes, and the hair already acting up so soon after she'd washed, dried, and carefully brushed it. But something about the tunic's color—and the way the garments fit her changing body rather than fighting it—had Mranes wondering where the nearly grown woman staring back at her had come from.

Several thick candles lit the gathering shelter, built of pale blue wood that had withstood both sun's heat and driving storms for years. Enough seating for their whole extended family and a few friends could be arranged inside.

Tonight only three chairs and a long, low sofa waited, all fitted with overstuffed yellow cushions. A little square table in the middle held more candles, their cheery flames dancing in the breeze, and the delicate blue pitcher and cups only brought out for celebrations.

Her parents waited as well, both of them dressed in clothing as fine as hers. Her mother's hair was more carefully braided than what she did for a typical day at sea, with strands of sparkling stones worked through it, along with several of the huge phertecha flowers.

She wore a sea-green dress, flowing around her arms and legs like the tide coming in back on the beach. Her father's rich brown tunic and breeches were a perfect match for the dress and his own hair and eyes.

Her mother walked toward her, and Mranes was startled to notice they stood nearly eye-to-eye after her latest burst of growing taller.

"You're simply lovely," she said, taking Mranes's hand. "So like your father with your long legs."

"And like your mother, with your glorious waves of hair," her father said. "Come join us and we'll speak of your sleeping lifetimes."

Mranes sank into one of the cushions on the sofa that looked like sunshine and felt like a cloud, trying her best not to get too nervous or so overly curious that she did nothing but ask questions rather than listening.

She fell into that habit more than she liked to admit.

Her parents sat on either side of her, silent and unmoving long enough that Mranes was certain they were testing to see how long she'd wait to say something.

She made it about three breaths, which she thought was quite good on a night like this.

"Thank you for the beautiful tunic and skirt, and especially the breeches. Are they special for recovering sleeping lifetimes?"

The amused glance her parents shared convinced Mranes they had been waiting for her to speak, but she found she didn't mind once *they* started speaking.

"They're special for *you,* love," her father said. "Nothing special is needed for recovering your sleeping lifetimes, except a person with the talent and skill."

"And most importantly," her mother said, "your willingness to have those lifetimes recovered. The lives lived behind our closed eyes are private and sacred to us, as they are to all people. Even those who dismiss them as mere dreams. But sometimes we prefer to leave those lifetimes in the shadows rather than bringing them into the light. So it must always be your choice."

Mranes felt warmth rush to her cheeks, remembering flashes of dreams she'd had about boys and girls in Gartria, and often about the most fascinating visitors. Recalling those more clearly might be exciting, and absolutely private.

But she didn't want her parents to know she had such thoughts awake or asleep.

"Can I recover a lifetime without telling someone else about it?"

Her mother's knowing smile and raised eyebrow made Mranes blush even deeper.

"With practice, yes, though it is more difficult. You always have the choice to say you want to stop, even once we begin. For lifetimes that are dark or frightening, you may decide you've relived enough to learn and understand. Or that you no longer want to. Both are valid choices."

"What you must always remember," her father said, "is

once you recall a sleeping lifetime, it won't fade away into the mist of sleep as it did the first time. That lifetime will take its place in your mind alongside your waking memories, with all the same vividness and emotion. Consider this before you move forward."

Mranes blurted out a question without thinking, which likely surprised neither of her parents.

"Can I recover my *own* dream lifetimes, then, without help? If I do want to keep them private, or want to make up my mind later?"

Her mother shook her head with a sad smile.

"I've never known anyone who could, though I'd guess all of us wish to. You may be able to help others recover theirs. I'd say odds are good for you, since both your father and I have the talent for it."

"Is that why no one talks about it?" Mranes said. "*Really* talks about it, I mean, to people my age? Because not everyone can do it?"

Mranes's father sat forward and poured dark liquid into three of the blue cups.

"That's part of the reason. Also because it's best to have some measure of maturity before those with the ability begin to learn how. An understanding of when to recover a lifetime, when not to, and how to keep anything revealed of that lifetime secret. Do you believe you're ready?"

He held out one of the cups to Mranes and one to her mother. Mranes held hers in both hands, the smooth ceramic cool against her palms. She smelled tart fruit juice, but with a sharper aroma she couldn't identify.

"I think I'm ready," she said. "What kind of lifetime will we recover? One of the frightening ones?"

Her mother smiled and brushed back the hair already twisting itself into disorder against Mranes's face.

"Any kind you wish as you learn more. It will be our joy

and honor to teach you as much as you want. But tonight, on the eve of your fourteenth birthday, the tradition is to seek the dreaming lifetime that reveals what you most desire in your waking lifetime."

Chills rippled along Mranes's arms and legs, and she was certain her unruly hair was trying to stand on end.

She'd heard older children in the village talking endlessly about what they were going to do when they grew up. Some spoke with rock-solid certainty of leaving. Of boarding one of the day-boats, or setting out on foot, or on a sturdy landhorse. Turning their eyes away from the seaside land of their birth and beginning their lives elsewhere.

Others never mentioned such adventurous notions, even in passing. They were set on learning a craft or a trade, and many began those pursuits not long after they had fourteen years. Going to sea like her mother, creating art like her father, or more practical things to offer to visitors or merchants.

Mranes had often wondered how people not much older than she had such clear ideas of the path they wanted to set foot on. And how they all seemed to do exactly that in the beginning, even if they decided to change course later in life.

But she'd caught brief flashes and bits of herself doing so many different things when her eyes were closed, both here and in places she'd never seen or heard of. Almost all of them things she didn't want to spend her whole life caught up in.

The visions and vivid sensations of herself in flight aboard a spectacular airhorse seemed rare and few compared to so much *ordinary*.

A cold, deep certainty that her mind would betray her rose up and gripped her heart.

"Can I change my mind later?" she said, unable to stop the trembling in her voice. "No matter what my sleeping lifetime holds?"

Her father tilted his head, a tiny frown on his lips and between his eyebrows.

"You're not bound by this, no. Most children see this as a good thing, a way to know their own hearts and minds and made their decisions from that knowledge. But you don't have to recover these lifetimes at all if you don't wish it."

Her mother put her cup down and moved closer to Mranes, one arm around her shoulder.

"Are you afraid, Mranes? Does something about this worry you?"

Mranes nodded, but she couldn't speak until she took a couple of deep breaths.

"What if the sleeping lifetime is *wrong*? What if the one we recover tonight isn't the right one? What if it's the *worst* one, something I never want to do?"

"We all have dreams of no real consequence," her father said. "The ones that fade away entirely, or only come back to us in bits and pieces. Part of the magic of recalling our sleeping lifetimes consciously, with a specific intention, is those random dreams fall to the wayside. And even with all of that, remember you always have the choice, love."

With a quick squeeze, Mranes's mother moved away and picked up her cup again.

"Knowing you as I do," she said, "I expect your mind and your heart will be aligned in this, as they so often are. And that you'll be wise and courageous enough to make the right decision no matter what."

Mranes gazed at one of the candles on the table, watching the way the flame swayed one direction, then another. Extending itself long and tall, then flattening to nearly nothing.

Adjusting itself to the breeze without ever detaching itself from the wick.

Moving freely, while still holding on to its foundation.

"I'd like to find out what my sleeping lifetimes hold."

Both of her parents nodded and smiled, and a bit of the fear lifted from her belly and chest.

"I've given you lacien juice," her father said. "The same thing we often drink when our bodies or minds feel as if they're drowning in trouble. Up until now, you've only had it watered down. This isn't the full potency your mother and I drink, sometimes before sleeping, often when we recover sleeping lifetimes for each other. But this is far stronger than you've ever tasted before."

Mranes raised the cup to her nose, taking a quick, cautious sniff.

"Is anything else in it? Something that smells so sharp?"

Her mother nodded and smiled. "We also hold some of the lacien juice back each year, and mix it with sweeter fruit and honey. Over time, the character changes and strengthens. Similar to the wine or beer I'm sure you've seen visitors and traders drinking, and I suspect you've tasted for yourself. But this is much stronger, so be prepared."

"Again, you have a *small* dose," her father said, tilting his head with a mock-stern expression. "Mainly to celebrate this special night. But some do intentionally drink it to explore their sleeping lifetimes more deeply, or before they sleep if they have a specific need they wish to pursue behind their closed eyes."

A thrill of curiosity drifted through Mranes at the idea of a deep dive into her sleeping lifetimes, chasing the last of her fear away. She raised her cup when her mother and father did, then watched as they raised theirs to their lips.

Once she saw they slowly drank the whole thing, she did the same.

The lacien juice was thicker than she'd tasted before, with a wonderful sweetness under the tart flavor. And a tingling burn whispered along her tongue and throat as she swal-

KARI KILGORE

lowed, settling into her belly like the comfort of a fire against the fierce chill of a winter storm.

Her mother leaned forward to set the empty cup on the table, and Mranes and her father did the same.

"What I remember from this night with my parents," her mother said, "is my arms and legs felt like they could float away. Like drifting in the shallows of the sea on a hot day."

Mranes tried to stop it, but a laugh escaped her anyway. That exact feeling was extending from the warmth in her belly throughout her whole body. She covered her mouth with one hand, but her father gently pulled it away.

"No, don't try to hide your laughter, your delight. This is a joyful thing, this passage. A little sad for us to be sure, but still wonderful to see. Your mother often lies with her head in my lap, and I do the same with her."

Mranes nodded, and her parents shifted to the ends of the sofa. After considering for a second, she stretched out with her head in her mother's lap, her feet in her father's.

One huge breath in and a sigh back out, her chest moving as the sea with the tides, and she closed her eyes.

She didn't feel especially sleepy, but now the cushions under her back truly did feel like a cloud. Her mother's voice drifted to her ears just as softly.

"You can learn about the lives lived behind your eyes for years, if you wish it. We'll teach you as much as we're able, and as truly as we can. Then if you still want more, we'll help you find your next teachers. But for now, we're searching for the desires of your heart."

"Your heart will have many desires over the years of your life." Her father rubbed her feet, soothing and calming. "More than you can yet imagine. We seek the desire *for* your life now. The path you wish to set your feet upon as you walk into adulthood."

Her mother brushed her hair back again, the sensation coming from a long way away.

"Listen to the beat of your heart now," she said. "The same heart that stays with you through all of your sleeping lifetimes, and every day you live and breathe in this world. Follow that sound, that rhythm. Your heart was the first part of you to come to life, so it knows you better than your mind ever could."

The slow, steady sound of her heart rose in Mranes's mind. Changing from something she never heard and seldom paid attention to into her entire focus. The beats even and reliable, so much so that counting them felt like a dreadful waste of time.

Those beats would be there, day after day, waking and sleeping. As long as she drew breath.

But right now, her mind drew her inward, where she could *see* her heart's beating rather than only hearing and feeling it.

Only the change from darkness to a flash of light at first.

Then shifting into streaks of movement.

Not quite like the flow of blood inside her, or out of her during her courses of womanhood.

This soared and dove, charging ahead and drifting feather-light.

Not only the black of her closed eyes and the red of her blood, but taking on all the colors she'd ever seen in all her lifetimes.

The movement concentrated, turning into a feeling to go with sound and sight.

Now Mranes soared herself, her stomach dropping and her mind and heart caught up in the thrill of motion.

The warmth in her belly solidified beneath her legs and hands, turning firm and substantial.

Her vision burst into full, glorious life.

She was *flying*, but not in the oddly detached sense of those nonsense dreams.

Mranes felt the wind against her face, heard it rush past her ears.

She crouched low against the huge, strong neck of an airhorse.

Her magnificent rainbow wings tucked close against her broad shoulders as she dove through the clouds, and the deep green trees and jagged black rocks of an unfamiliar mountain range exploded into view.

The vision shifted, and now the airhorse flew at a pace as steady and strong as Mranes's heartbeat, while the land below rippled in red and orange and yellow, without a cloud or anything else besides *dry* in sight. Mranes felt her skin tighten, her mouth and throat grow parched. She somehow knew the desert below her was harsh and unforgiving, even as she recognized its beauty.

Then she flew in formation with a dozen other airhorses, their wings and manes and tails flashing in colors she'd never seen with her eyes open before. And they flew over a great city full of buildings of every shape and size, with a sea rough and gray stretching out in the distance.

A sea nothing like the one she'd always known.

Mranes had no doubt that vast, choppy water was a long way from Gartria.

At that, the thrill of flight slipped away from her.

Rejoining her body felt like landing hard enough to knock the wind out of her chest.

She gasped and opened her eyes.

Her head still rested in the soft familiarity of her mother's lap, her feet warm in her father's. The shifting light of candles revealing her own yard and outdoor shelter.

The aroma of roasting fowl much stronger.

The slow, growling roar of the tide coming in not far away.

Safe within the home and family she now *knew* she'd be leaving behind.

Mranes sat up slowly, accepting a cup full of plain water from her father.

"You may feel a little dizzy, love. Take a drink and settle yourself in this world."

She swallowed the cool water, letting it replace the fading warmth of lacien juice all the way down.

"Not too dizzy," she said. "Not quite ready to go running down the beach yet either. I feel more...stiff than dizzy. Like I've been out here for hours."

Her mother laughed from beside her.

"Not hours, my dearest," she said. "But close to an hour."

Mranes let her father take the cup, then rubbed her face and stretched.

"Did I say anything?"

"No words, but I'm quite sure I heard you laughing." He gave her another cupful, and she drank it all again. "If you'd like, you can share your lifetime with us."

The fierce joy of flight battled with the sadness of leaving until Mranes thought it would drive her to tears. She hoped talking would settle her feelings down, or at least give her a better way to think about them.

"I think... No, I *know* the desire of my heart is to become an airhorse rider." She turned to her father. "I know they work terribly hard, and sometimes they get hurt." Then to her mother. "And I know I'll be a long, long way from here most of the time. That won't be easy, any of it."

Her mother didn't look upset or sad or even afraid. Instead she raised her chin with a proud gleam in her eye.

"And yet, it's what you *want*. You've never been the kind

of child to shy away from a thing because it was hard. That's one of the many things I love about you, Mranes."

"Think of it this way," her father said, and Mranes was sure she caught the sparkle of a tear in his eye. "Many people go far away from home and family. But very few can return for visits as easily as an airhorse rider."

Now Mranes blinked back tears of her own, but not of fear, or even of the homesickness sure to come.

"You think this sleeping lifetime spoke truly then? And you'll let me go?"

All at once, her parents both caught her in a great hug.

"You've daydreamed of this for years," her father said. "Your eyes drift skyward every chance you get. Even before you found this sleeping lifetime. I've always trusted you to know your own heart."

"Of course you can go, as long as you *do* take your chances to visit." Her mother kissed her cheek and sat back. "I'll want to make sure you're beaming with joy exactly as you are right now."

This time Mranes didn't even try to hold back the laughter dancing inside as she grasped her parents' hands.

"I'll never stay away too long, I promise. I may not have an airhorse yet, but my heart has wings already."

KARI KILGORE

AUTHOR OF ODDS AND ENDINGS AND THE EARWORMS

Footprints Along the Path

A MISFORTUNE AND MAGIC STORY

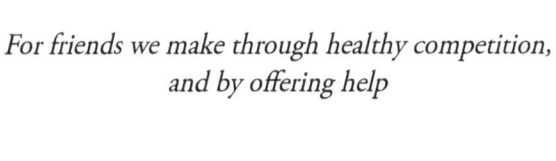

*For friends we make through healthy competition,
and by offering help*

Chapter 1

THE SMALL, stone Reflection Chamber normally felt comforting to Apprentice Goresi Awinish.

Barely four of her strides across in each direction, with only one window facing the red, orange, and purple of an autumn sunset. The rippled glass cast wavery light across the pale gray walls. A long, thin cushion covered with coarse brown fabric provided the only protection from the smooth blue stone of the floor.

Goresi had long ago figured out the trick of kneeling on the end of the cushion, then folding the rest behind her and over her heels, making a surprisingly comfortable prop for her backside. Not the height of luxury, perhaps, but infinitely better than trying to arrange herself any other way.

That pose left her pale-yellow apprentice robe in a half-circle around her, the soft wool drifting itself into tiny ridges and valleys. A temporary garment the color of her immature magic, the robe didn't have any of the elaborate embroidery that signified a full magc.

Those patterns in colorful and often metallic thread

transformed a simple garment into both a symbol and an actual object of power.

Like all unmarried women across the vast continent of Hanferthen, her hair fell loose and free past her shoulders. Her mother and sisters kept their own dark blonde waves bound, and expected Goresi to someday do the same.

Even before she'd left home to pursue her training, *she'd* expected to do otherwise.

The only other thing in the room when she'd walked in was a small bronze cup, and a rough ceramic pitcher full of Caderna: cool water drawn from deep beneath the plateau of Dirgelan. She'd never tasted water or anything else so sweet and complex, with a sharp mineral aftertaste that always left her wanting to drink more.

Or anything as deeply steeped in the power of the massive crystals and gems that drove so much of the study and use of magic that it glowed with its own faint rainbow shimmer.

Only mages and their apprentices drank Caderna, and only when they were in their high, arid city. Even nearing the end of her years of apprenticeship, Goresi hadn't begun to get used to the potent surge a single sip gave her.

Apprentices facing what they hoped was their final challenge—like Goresi—enjoyed an unlimited supply.

An array of small objects waited beside her, arranged on a circle of leather than matched her robe, even though she really shouldn't be using most of them right now.

A glittering array of gemstones of various shapes and sizes, all chips and fragments of the much larger stones deep under her feet.

Three candles about the same size as her thumb: one white, one black, one sparkling silver. Each produced a flame the same color as its wax, and played a different part in the rituals she'd practiced and repeated until they were natural as breathing.

A shallow copper bowl covered with the swoops and whorls of magical symbols she'd designed to expand her power. Practice work for designs she hoped to use on her proper mage robe in a few days' time.

Providing she chose new wool in the still-unknown color for her mature magic. From what she'd heard in the swirling mess of apprentice rumors, that wouldn't be nearly as simple as it sounded.

Making the wrong choice once could be forgiven with several months of further training and practice.

A second incorrect choice would be the end of her dreams of stepping into the world as an Honored Mage.

All of her tools paled beside the most important for the newest, raw apprentice or the most experienced, powerful Honored Mage. A colorless crystal the length of her longest finger, and narrow enough to fit comfortably into her palm.

Her Focus Stone.

A shard of the massive Elemental Crystal deep beneath Dirgelan.

A deeply sacred object she'd only behold for herself if she passed this final test.

Goresi picked up her Focus Stone and held it in her open hand. It lit with a warm, yellow glow, not much different than the sun growing ever closer to the rocky edge of the plateau.

Once it set completely and slipped out of sight, she'd be out of time.

And right now her mind wandered and jumped and jittered in a most undisciplined and frustrating manner.

She drew in a deep breath, reminding herself of her most unusual talent, one she hoped would serve her well as a full mage.

Assuming she managed to drag her focus and attention under control.

The thing that set her apart—and helped convince her parents and the teaching mages that she truly belonged here—was her ability to smell even the faintest trace of magic.

Right now she caught each individual gemstone, her Focus Stone, and the strong hit of Caderna. Lingering traces of mages and apprentices alike who'd spent time in this same room. A faint and ever-present touch of the magic of the plain of Dirgelan itself, woven into the plants and stone and the very air.

Not exactly as smells, like baking bread or fresh-turned soil or the herb and flower gardens close to the kitchens.

This was more a *sensation*.

A tingling shiver.

An idea of the color of the magic, and a sense of its strength.

Almost like a sound that set off an echoing, answering tone from her own magic deep inside.

Goresi had no idea how uncommon her ability was until she arrived in Dirgelan as an excited fifteen-year-old, after a walk of several months from her distant plains home of Hameatha.

That seemingly endless walk in the company of a traveling Honored Mage had given her a glimpse into the astonishing knowledge she would spend the next decade of her life devouring in every waking second, then practicing and contemplating even in her dreams.

She shook her head, frustrated at how her thoughts were once again wandering at will.

The whole purpose of this quiet time to herself in one of the city's many Reflection Chambers was to prepare for the evening's test. To ponder the lessons she'd learned, the discoveries she'd made in over ten years of intensive study and practice.

To bring those milestones into focus, observe them, and store them in the organized corners of her mind. Discover the meaning, let it direct her path toward what would allow her to best serve, while returning both pleasure and reward in that service.

So she could walk before the Council of Mages clear-headed, and emerge as a full mage herself.

She took a drink of Caderna, paying close attention to the way it refreshed her. Not only in her mouth and throat, cooling all the way down to her belly. It also provided a boost to her magic. One that promised to clear the jitteriness of her mind.

She'd already considered several of her more notorious exploits during her training. Accidentally discovering how to store her youthful, untrained magic in tiny silver baubles should have been the most important, or at least the most substantial. But that memory and the uncomfortable amount of attention that went with it only made her lack of focus worse.

"By all the powers that be," Goresi whispered, "I choose to control my mind, not be controlled by my careless thoughts."

And yet, in this case, she might need to let her instinctive magic take control instead of directing it.

Make her ever-active and always curious mind step aside for a change.

Another sip of Caderna, and the chance to inhale deeply of its rippling power.

Then Goresi clasped her Focus Stone in both hand and closed her eyes.

She followed the first ripple that rose to the calm surface of memories.

Chapter 2

If GORESI HAD to conjure one more glowing trail showing her own footprints, she was afraid she'd sit right down on the stony ground of the practice field and cry.

Possibly only the rough, uncomfortably bumpy reality of that ground beneath her sturdy leather boots stopped her from doing just that.

An expanse of the exposed rust-colored bedrock of the Dirgelan Plateau might make the perfect spot for illuminating a trail without the helpful use of mud, soft grass, or even much dust.

But trying to sit on it could only make the unpleasant business of feeling sorry for oneself worse, especially when not one person nearby would spare her an instant of sympathy.

She and a swarm of other apprentices—of various ages but similar levels of experience—had been repeating the words out loud, under their breath, and in their minds for what felt like hours.

But she knew the words themselves didn't matter, not once they were properly committed to memory.

The real key to conjurings and spells and enchantments was learning how to recreate the *feel* of the specific magic. To understand how this created a different sensation in her mind and through the Focus Stone in her hand than conjuring a rope of light.

Both involved creating a glow where one hadn't been before, yes.

Both helped with finding her way in a new place, which almost all of the vast city of Dirgelan still was to her, with its endless rows of streets and curving boulevards, packed full of buildings of every possible size, shape, and material.

But the energy of both a rope of light and a glowing tracery of her footsteps took up an entirely different space in her magic.

Goresi had shown an early knack for that idea for whatever reason, giving her perhaps an unfair advantage over apprentices sometimes ten years her senior at fifteen. During moments like this, when she struggled to keep from shouting out her frustration, she wondered if quick learning might be more of a *disadvantage* instead.

To distract herself while her fellow apprentices struggled, she concentrated on refining her conjuring. Playing with it, if she wanted to be honest.

She stood in a big rounded area to herself, like everyone did to keep from trampling over each others' paths. Unlike most of the others, Goresi's footprints still glowed in the eerie yellow they'd taken on almost at once, outlining the spiral pattern she'd walked within her practice space.

Glancing to her right, she caught sight of a brilliant pink robe without paying attention to who wore it. An easy push inward, and a careful adjustment to the feel of her conjuring, and Goresi's footprints took on the same pink while the circle next to hers remained bedrock rust with nothing illuminated at all, no matter how hard the apprentice there swore.

She did the same with pale blue, deepest black, and a rich burgundy. Then she worked through sparkling gold, silver, and copper, before turning each of her prints into a different color at the same time.

A prickly aroma of delicately sweet magic alerted her before someone spoke.

"How did you *do* that?"

She turned to see a short, slender girl in the practice circle next to hers, with a head full of thick brown hair floating in the breeze. The girl's robe was an intense, rich orange. Only a couple of matching footprint shapes marked the ground around her.

Her pale blue eyes were wide, but thank all the powers that be, her expression was more curious and admiring than upset.

"I just...well, I figured out how to change the color is all."

Goresi knew her cheeks were flaming red, but she wasn't sure why or what to do about it.

She hadn't meant to show off or make anyone else feel bad. With an older brother, two older sisters, and more younger siblings, she was much too familiar with that kind of teasing behavior to want to pass it along to a stranger.

A stranger who grinned and mouthed a silent *wow* as she took a few steps closer.

Steps that didn't show up on the ground at all.

"I'm only getting a few of my footprints to light up, and not for very long. Yours look like *paintings* or something, they're so vivid. I'm Machia, by the way. Did you learn how to do that before you got here?"

Goresi smiled at the energetic burst of conversation, more than she'd heard since leaving home. The Honored

Mage she'd apprenticed herself to, a kind man called Dawelan, had rarely spoken above a soothing tone.

So different from the rowdy, strong-willed, *loud* family she'd grown up in that it took weeks for Goresi to believe he wouldn't snap at her for asking her never-ending stream of questions.

Still, she'd asked him along the way how he could stand to work with clueless apprentices, answering the same questions and teaching the same history and basic skills over and over again.

He'd smiled in his gentle way and replied as he often did.

Saying Goresi would understand in due time, and most assuredly when she least expected it.

"This is all new," she said, waving a hand toward her footprints and adjusting them back to the yellow of her robe. "It just made sense to me is all. I'm sure there are conjurings that you'll pick up with no trouble at all, too."

Machia brightened and started to speak, but a sharper voice cut in first.

"Wasting your time with that one. I haven't caught her doing much of anything. Not the right way at least."

Another girl, this one wearing a gray robe so pale Goresi wasn't sure if it was more blue or purple, stood at the edge of her practice circle with her arms crossed. She looked several years older, and her frown overwhelmed everything else about her face.

Her footprints stood out clear and sharp-edged in an intricate pattern that looked like one half of a dance.

"Thank you for the information," Goresi said in her best dismissive tone. "We'll continue our conversation now."

She turned her back toward the rude girl and motioned for Machia to do the same. The flash of gratitude in Machia's eyes helped soothe Goresi's pounding heart.

Another lesson she'd learned in her large family was confrontation with someone older rarely ended well.

And as often happened in her family, the first attempt to avoid trouble failed.

"I'm quite sure I remember the Honored Mages telling us not to help each other," the older girl said. "Maybe you weren't paying attention, same as when they told us not to try to do more than what we're *supposed* to be practicing."

Machia didn't turn around, but her face crumpled into fear.

Goresi did turn. And she sent her own footprints cycling through all the colors of the rainbow and more.

"I remember the Honored Mages telling us to respect each other's experience level, *and* our own," she said. "And what they actually said was to do each new task for ourselves so we could learn. Seems to me that's what *you* should concentrate on."

She leaned closer to Machia, shaking her head and looking into her eyes. Goresi ignored the way her own hands were shaking.

"Don't pay any attention to her. She's just trying to upset you. One of my brothers is the same way. I used to pretend he was inside a box made of mirrors talking to himself. Since he loves nothing more than himself and the sound of his own voice, he'd be quite happy in there."

Machia giggled, then covered her mouth to try to muffle the sound.

The older girl only raised her voice. Another of the tricks Goresi's brother used to get their parents' attention without openly asking for it.

Usually when he didn't like something his brothers or sisters were doing.

"I hardly think you're best to help someone who's having

so much trouble. It's not like you're one of the teaching mages. Or likely to ever become one."

As she often did when faced with taunting from her brother, Goresi wished the box of mirrors was real. Or at the very least that she could put a mirrored wall between the two of them so he'd mind his own affairs and leave her alone.

But for the first time, she made that wish with her magic at the front of her mind rather than lurking mysterious and unknown.

For the first time, Goresi had the ability—and the will—to change the situation for the better.

A small change, really.

Nothing more than making the boundaries of their practice circles match her desires.

She didn't quite direct the shift, but she did *feel* it.

Goresi had no idea her wish had made the jump to reality until Machia gasped, and the light behind them changed.

Heart pounding in her dry throat, Goresi looked over her shoulder.

And all she saw was herself and Machia, and all the apprentices behind them staring open-mouthed.

What looked like a curved wall of reflective glass blocked the rude girl from sight. Goresi couldn't tell if it went all the way around, but the lack of the now-invisible girl's voice raised in protest or any other sound gave her a strong hint.

The way all sound and motion on the practice plain stopped confirmed her suspicion.

Now *everyone* stared.

Despite her alarm when she caught sight of more than one Honored Mage heading her way, Goresi noticed right away how the apprentices around her were smiling.

A full mage in a beautifully embroidered robe the deep

red of thunderclouds at sunset arrived first, her face set in a well-practiced scowl.

The fierce expression didn't reach Mage Hathren's twinkling eyes.

"Quite an impressive display, Apprentice Goresi." She glanced at Goresi's multi-colored footprints, then turned her attention to the mirrored wall. "We'll expect a full explanation of how you conjured such a thing, once you've endured my rather extensive explanation of how dangerous untested, uncontrolled magic can be."

Goresi lowered her head, partly to hide her smile as several men and women in full mage robes gathered, each appearing to examine their reflections in the wall.

The lecture was sure to be dire. But knowing she'd somehow managed something the teaching mages hadn't expected made it all worthwhile.

"Yes, Honored Mage. I'm terribly sorry for lashing out."

"We'll also discuss that in great detail later, I assure you. Now, kindly remove your conjuring."

A jagged, red-hot jolt of fear left Goresi trembling and covered in sweat.

What if she couldn't?

What if all they could do was break the glass, and hope the girl inside was unharmed?

What if it was a *solid* block of glass?

What if she tried to remove it, and it collapsed on itself?

And not even the powerful Honored Mages skilled in healing could undo the damage?

Her throat clicked loud in her ears when she tried to swallow.

Whether the glass was solid or not, now Goresi's mind surely was. As solid and hard and unmovable as the stone beneath her feet.

A small, cool hand slipped into hers.

Goresi's neck creaked with tension when she turned to look down at Machia. Her grateful smile let Goresi's frozen mind relax enough to lurch and sputter back into life.

She still *felt* the change in her magic that created the wall. The shift.

All she had to do was return back to before she made that change.

"Yes, Honored Mage."

When the wall disappeared—revealing the now red-faced and furious girl inside—Goresi's breath left her body in a great whoosh.

Red-robed Mage Hathren nodded, and a hint of a smile crossed her face.

"Very well. Apprentice Machia, would you like Apprentice Goresi to practice tracing footsteps with you? That and *not one thing* more?"

Machia bobbed down into a nervous bow, nodding the whole time.

"Yes Honored Mage, very much so."

"Then you may work together during the time we have left this morning." She turned to intercept the angry girl, who'd recovered enough to stride forward with her fists clenched. "Apprentice Egwen, I believe you would like me to review the procedures for apprentices assisting one another? And perhaps explain the meaning of respecting your various levels of experience in magical practice? In rather excruciating detail?"

Egwen stopped, and her face flushed bright red. But Goresi had to admit she was impressed at how quickly Egwen first unknotted her fists to smooth her gray robe, then folded them together across her stomach.

She might be one worth getting to know, once they'd each endured their lectures.

"Yes, Honored Mage," Egwen said, lowering her gaze. "I

appreciate the opportunity to learn, as always." She shot a heated glance at Goresi. "And to teach."

"I'm filled with joy to hear it," Mage Hathren said, with her half-smile firmly in place as she raised her voice. "Now, all of you, continue your practice. This may seem like a mundane and disappointing use of your budding magical skills. But *do* consider how useful the ability to retrace your steps would be in a situation far less friendly than the sanctuary of the Dirgelan Plateau."

She and the other full mages paused, then walked away in different directions, as if responding to a signal invisible to mere apprentices.

Goresi suspected she wasn't the only one who very much wanted to know how they did that. Machia squeezed her hand before she let go.

"What you said earlier?" she said in a quiet voice. "About how I'd pick up some conjurings without any trouble at all? Remember?"

Goresi glanced at Egwen, and she was more relieved than she wanted to admit to see nothing but her stiff and angry back.

"I remember," Goresi said.

Machia looked around, then leaned closer.

"Watch," she whispered.

Goresi raised her head to keep her focus on Machia's face before she realized what she was doing. Rather than standing around shoulder height, now Machia faced her eye-to-eye. When Goresi managed to look down, Machia's feet floated several inches off the blue stone of the practice ground.

She grinned and settled herself to the ground before Goresi got words from her mind to her open mouth.

"You *have* to tell me how you *did* that."

"I will. I promise."

Chapter 3

GORESI OPENED her eyes just as the last sliver of the fiery red sun disappeared below the distant edge of the Dirgelan Plateau.

Her mind now as calm as her body after a much-needed time of stillness.

She conjured a glowing yellow rope along the blue stone floor of the Reflection Chamber, just bright enough so she could gather her tools. She slipped her gemstones, the unlit candles, her carefully etched copper bowl, and the circle of leather into her yellow robe's many pockets.

When she lifted the coarse ceramic pitcher, she was surprised at how light it was.

She'd drunk most of the power-infused Caderna drawn from deep beneath her feet without realizing it. With a grin and a shrug, she poured the last into the bronze cup.

The tingle of magic from her lips and tongue and down into her throat and belly was as strong as ever.

She'd never quite gotten the hang of Machia's easy levita-tion, no matter how hard she tried over the years. Thank all the powers that be, Machia never tired of practicing with her, or endlessly talking over everything they learned.

Machia had picked up the trick of illuminating her footsteps, but without Goresi's color-changing flair.

She got easily to her feet, stretching her legs as she flattened the thin mat and left it against the wall. Honored Mages were allowed thick cushions and even chairs when they used the Reflection Chambers, and assured the apprentices that they'd appreciate the option once they had endless miles under their feet, or under their backsides if they traveled by landhorse or airhorse.

Goresi wondered whether Egwen had finished her own final test. After over ten years as friendly rivals and reliable competitors, neither were surprised to reach that milestone on the same evening.

As she walked toward the wooden door and extinguished her rope of light, Goresi finally noticed the warm glow of her Focus Stone in her right hand.

The yellow shone strongest, as it had since the day she first brought it to life.

But now ripples of deep purple moved underneath, like the tide coming in by the light of the full moons.

That could be nothing but the color of her mature magic breaking through at last.

Her joyful laughter echoed off the stone walls before she went out to face her final test, confident she'd emerge on the other side as Honored Mage Goresi.

And eventually walk away from the Dirgelan Plateau in richly embroidered robes of that lovely purple.

Leaving glowing footprints along the path of her own best destiny.

KARI KILGORE

AUTHOR OF ODDS AND ENDINGS AND THE EARWORMS

Trusting Their Magic

A MISFORTUNE AND MAGIC STORY

For all of us who've learned about ourselves
with the help of a four-legged companion

TRUSTING THEIR MAGIC

EVEN AFTER NEARLY TWO months of spending hours with them every day, a huge group of airhorses still took Tonn Groyen's breath. Especially when they flew riderless and free overhead, stretching out their wings before a day of hard work.

They wheeled and spun, weaving through the air in great patterns that reminded him of the vast machines that made the woolen parts of the uniform he wore. His jacket and breeches were a nondescript tan like all the other riders-in-training, with matching leather added where the clothes took a lot of abuse. They all carried helmets and wore boots in the same drab shade.

One of the best parts about finally being paired with his own airhorse rather than the constant changes of training would be having riding gear made to match. That small change would drop the possibility of blending in with other riders to non-existent.

Because the soaring creatures maneuvering so joyfully against the clear blue autumn sky sported all the colors Tonn knew the names for and more. Sunflower yellow, blood red, rich pumpkin orange. Brilliant pink, springtime green, and blue deeper than the sky.

An equal number of rich chestnut, gleaming white, or earthy brown joined in, not quite as dazzling but no less beautiful in the sky.

Most of their manes and tails showed different colors from their bodies, completing the dazzling display.

The sunlight passed through the thin, furry membrane of their broad wings as they glided, highlighting the jewel-like tones even more.

Tonn stood in his base group of other young riders, most of them somewhere around their middle teen years. They'd all started their training together barely sixty days ago, right before he'd reached his fifteenth year.

Sometimes the passing time felt like years, others like only he'd only arrived the day before.

A brisk autumn wind stirred up the short lavender grass of the practice field, carrying the scent of cooking fires all across the hilly, curving streets of Maestar. Tonn couldn't imagine visiting them all, but he'd already discovered a dizzying array of taverns among row after row of stone, brick, and wooden buildings.

When he didn't feel adventurous enough to sample food from all across the great continent of Hanferthen, or when he didn't want to part with the meager supply of coin he earned in allowance as part of his training, ordinary but filling meals in the lodging house he shared with other trainees sufficed.

As a city devoted entirely to airhorses and their riders, especially with big portions of each still young and growing, keeping everyone fed in Maestar was a constant occupation.

Sometimes Tonn wasn't sure whether his fellow trainees or the group of yearling airhorses they were getting to know grew faster or ate more. He'd sprouted up noticeably since leaving home himself, after constantly feeling like the shortest boy in any room for years.

He was still shorter than almost everyone in their group —including the girls—but at long last he was gaining ground.

Right now his red hair was in the midst of growing past his chin: the longest he'd ever worn it. The farming community he'd come from in Hameatha kept far stricter customs for such things than the city of airhorses. He was nowhere near the only young rider—male or female—enjoying a huge expansion of their freedoms in Maestar.

Tonn was also far from the only one with what even he admitted was a *disorganized* appearance.

Questionable as those choices might be, as long as it didn't interfere with their training or safety, the most the stable masters did was smile and shake their heads.

And of course the freedom of appearance or clothing or pretty much anything else fell away compared to the incredible thought of someday escaping into the sky with his own airhorse.

Free to go as he chose, many times faster and easier than the landbound limited to walking, riding a landhorse, or sailing the great and dangerous seas.

Well, free within reason, and according to the duty that would come along with his final airhorse match.

Tonn glanced at the stable master for his base group, standing off to the side, hands jammed firmly on her curving hips.

Stable Master Adur Helander wore the same scarlet as her huge airhorse William, and her close-cropped silver hair sparkled in the sun. She watched the aerial display as intently as the riders-in-training did, but Tonn had no doubt she saw a thousand little details he hadn't even learned to look for yet.

Master Adur never tired of reminding Tonn and all the other new riders to "Eat eat *eat*, but never forget to feed and care for your airhorse first!"

None of Tonn's group had their permanent airhorses yet, so that meant many hours spent feeding, washing, and brushing the stable full of yearlings, and sometimes helping out with injured or retired beasts as well.

Since the airhorses all carried pleasant smells nearly as varied as their colors, Tonn considered time spent with them a small price to pay for the joy of flight.

He jumped at Master Adur's sharp voice.

"How did they learn the flight pattern we're observing right now? Tonn?"

He was certain he knew the answer, but a rush of nerves sent his belly twisting anyway.

"Same way landhorses do, or fish or fowl or anything else, Master. They're playing. Or at least that's how it starts out."

"Exactly so." Master Adur's warm smile balanced out her sometimes-harsh tones and fierce expressions. "The wild colony of airhorses not far from here does much the same every morning when the weather's fair. Have any of you had a chance to observe them in their own play?"

Every hand shot up.

Tonn took every chance he got to take the long walk out past Maestar's towering city wall, cutting through the low passage out to the rocky cliffs overlooking the sea. He often joined an awe-struck crowd who also made the trip by the faintest light of dawn, hoping to catch a display even more breathtaking than the one over their heads.

When the wild colony greeted the new day, dancing through the air without any of the routines or discipline working airhorses picked up over the years.

Master Adur glanced skyward again, where the airhorses

were finally taking on the long, slow glide pattern toward the ground.

When she looked back, she had a wicked gleam in her wide brown eyes.

"Any of you know why we have the wild colony? Why we don't simply tame all of them instead?"

This time the group of trainees managed to stare everywhere but back at their stable master, Tonn included. He and probably all the rest of them knew the answer, and had almost since the day they arrived in Maestar.

The whispered gossip and intensely curious discussions about *this* topic never seemed to stop.

But Tonn wasn't sure any of them would have the courage, or the confidence, to say it out loud.

Then one raised her hand, and Tonn wasn't all that surprised after all. Mranes not only seemed to do the work of three when it came to feeding and grooming time, she also seemed to know nearly as much as Master Adur or any of their other teachers.

Even without all that and wearing the same tan clothing, Mranes was too striking to overlook all on her own. She stood several inches taller than Tonn, and her brown skin and curls almost the same color were most unusual compared to where he came from. Almost everyone in Hameatha had the same pale skin as Tonn, and either red or blond hair.

Here he'd joined trainees with much darker skin, or a reddish or blueish hue.

He'd caught sight of an unforgettable rider with *violet* skin and sky blue hair a few days before, and she'd even worn the brilliant flowing robe of an Honored Mage.

"Maestar's wild colony is primarily for breeding, Master Adur," Mranes said, "especially for their first time. That helps keep our airhorses healthy and strong."

The rosy flush Tonn saw in Mranes's cheeks only made

her more appealing, but the way she held her chin high kept him from even thinking about telling her so.

Master Adur raised one eyebrow and nodded at the same time, again with her encouraging smile.

"That's correct, Mranes. Anyone care to explain why that makes a difference?"

Tonn was distantly shocked to hear his own voice, and he was certain his blush wouldn't be anywhere near as pleasant to look at as Mranes's was.

"We do that with landhorses were I grew up, or *they* did. My family does. Making sure they don't pass along bad traits, I mean. Sometimes they rotate out animals with other families for that reason. We also did with cattle and fowl, and I know sheep and such, they're the same."

The too-fast jumble of words finally registered with Tonn's ears, and he was sure they would burst from the rush of heat.

Thank all the powers that be, Master Adur only nodded and smiled again.

"You have it, Tonn. Our long tradition of having male and female airhorses mate with the wild colony helps keep weakness from building up in either group over time, and brings strength and vitality for all the airhorses. And to be blunt, I believe letting these somewhat tame beasts spend time with their wild mates does their hearts and minds a world of good."

She looked over her shoulder where they'd now landed, and Mranes took the opportunity to grin at Tonn.

Who promptly blushed even harder.

"Now, they're warmed up and ready," Master Adur said, "and I saw no signs of soreness or injury in their flight. We'll learn more about how to watch for that in the weeks ahead. Airhorse yearlings do their best to hide their injuries or physical difficulties so they won't be grounded, much like two-legged trainees do. Both with roughly equal measures of success. For now, you're off for your morning flights."

Everyone headed toward the airhorses, now prancing and stretching their wings at the other end of the vast practice field. A thick line of trees marked the far edge where it butted up against two more for older trainees perfecting more difficult skills than Tonn's group had yet been allowed to attempt.

That tree-lined boundary marked the sharp lines that every trainee knew must be respected at all times, walking or flying. Even the airhorses seemed to understand that rule. Crossing into another group's practice field was certain to get a rider-in-training grounded for a painfully long time, and no possibility of talking their way out of it.

Only Mranes called out a question.

"Any instructions on which airhorses we should ride this morning, Master Adur?"

All the trainees stopped, and Tonn was sure he wasn't the only one wondering why *they* hadn't asked. They'd been rotating since their first day, giving themselves and the airhorses a wide range of practice in different combinations. Usually following the suggestions of the nearest stable master.

Master Adur's smile broadened.

"I expect many of you have grown fond of one beast over the last several weeks?" She paused while Tonn, Mranes, and everyone else nodded. "Then choose on that basis. If you can't work out any disputes, ask me or another stable master for guidance. But *do* try to work it out yourselves first. Or let the airhorses decide for you. You'll soon learn to trust their good judgement in many things. And their magic."

That set off a flurry of curious and excited conversation. Tonn still knew almost nothing of the world of magic, and the striking blue-skinned rider he'd spotted was the first time he could remember seeing an Honored Mage. But all of the trainees were thrilled with the idea of airhorses having magic beyond what let them fly every bit as well as any great hunting bird.

Tonn was delighted and only a little bit frightened when Mranes fell into step beside him. The fact that she had such a sweet and friendly disposition to go with her intelligence and beauty somehow made her *more* intimidating, at least to him.

"Have a favorite picked out yet, Tonn?"

He glanced at her, hoping desperately that they hadn't grown attached to the same airhorse.

"There's one the orange of a fine autumn squash who seems to like me. His hooves, mane, and tail are as blue as the sky right now."

Her eyes caught the morning sunlight, and he noticed how bright green they were.

"Oh, he's a beauty. Nice and solid, too, and steady in the air."

Tonn chewed his cheek for a second before he spoke.

"What about you? Which is your favorite?"

Mranes looked ahead, then pointed.

"See the indigo with her wings up just now?"

He gasped at the sight. The intensely colored deep blue wings stretched much higher than the others around her, and her broad back did as well. Unlike most of the others, she was the same vibrant color all over.

She was also one of the few yearlings who'd scared him in the air more than he wanted to admit.

"That one is beautiful too. I think she's the fastest of all the ones I've ridden."

Mranes flashed a grin he could only describe as fierce.

"She *is* the fastest, and she turns like a whip in midair. I've watched her with other riders in our group. I'm nowhere near as good as Master Adur at knowing what to look for in airhorses, but I'm sure that one flies differently with me. Like she knows I'm not afraid."

Relief that Mranes wasn't eyeing the handsome orange airhorse whirled with even more respect for her fearlessness in Tonn's mind.

"Sounds like how Master Orya talked about wing captains and their airhorses," he said. "The ones who have to keep everyone organized on big flights and do inspections and assign duties and all."

Mranes shrugged. "That wouldn't be so bad. I had a lot of practice keeping other kids focused while I was growing up. I'll have to tell you how we all had to work together on our pier sometime. Do you want to be wing captain too?"

Tonn considered lying, but only for a second. She'd asked without a trace of teasing or mean-spirit.

And he didn't want her to recommend him to any of the stable masters for that vital role. Mranes seemed like the kind of person who'd do that.

Worse when it came to the thought of being wing captain himself, he suspected the masters would listen to her.

"I don't think I'd like that as much," he said. "I like working with a group but not telling everyone what to do. That's not... I didn't mean it to sound bad, I just... I'd rather know what I'm supposed to do instead of having to decide for everyone all the time."

Mranes nodded, her delicate features serious, and still not teasing or mean.

"That's important, knowing what you like. My mother is a fisher down in Genfrith where I'm from, with several boats in her fleet. She says the Wrynath Sea is calm and gentle compared to the cold ones up here in the north. But *any* sea will still take you under if everyone doesn't know their role and enjoy doing it. No ship can sail without her crew."

Before Tonn could decide if he was more impressed by

her words or the ringing tone of her voice when she said them, colorful movement ahead caught his eye.

The gorgeous indigo airhorse let out a low chuffing nicker and turned her huge head to the side...right toward the pumpkin orange one. Tonn held his breath, and managed not to sigh out loud when the two of them touched noses, blew out loud enough that he heard it, then moved to stand side by side.

"They like each other," he said under his breath, but not as quietly as he thought.

"I was hoping that's what it meant," Mranes said. "Much as I love flying, I'm still learning their language. You grew up around them?"

Tonn shook his head, keeping his eye on a tall blond boy he'd only spoken to a couple of times walking toward the orange airhorse.

Most of the other trainees and airhorses alike had spread out on the practice field, pairing off as they went. None of them were allowed to get anywhere near a saddle before they did a physical inspection to make sure the airhorses really were sound to fly.

Since the stable masters looked them over as well, Tonn knew the trainee inspection was more for practice. But he'd never dare skip it.

"I didn't grow up with airhorses," he said, "but around lots of landhorses. They work on the farms and help carry the harvest in for trading. So far they seem to have pretty similar habits."

A beautiful charcoal gray with violet accents headed toward their little group with a bouncy gait, shaking his head and folding his wings as he went. He was well-made and nimble in the air, and a real pleasure to fly.

But like Tonn, he was the smallest of the three.

"I didn't see landhorses or airhorses very often at all when

I was growing up." Mranes stopped before they reached the beasts, crossing her arms. "One sight of an airhorse in flight was enough for me. You go ahead."

She nodded toward the blond boy, now reaching toward the orange airhorse's nose with a gentle hand. Tonn watched the indigo airhorse step to the side with her head held high as he walked.

He had the strangest feeling she would have her arms crossed like Mranes if she'd been able.

"Morning Tonn," the boy called, and Tonn remembered speaking to him a few times.

He cast about for his name, but for a few frantic seconds all he could remember was the boy being a couple of years older than the other trainees. Tonn wasn't sure whether to be friendly or cold to someone who seemed to be cutting in on the airhorse he wanted for the morning.

Either would be silly and remarkably ineffective if he couldn't remember his *name*.

That annoying thought jarred his memory loose.

"Morning Soren. Good day for flying."

Soren glanced at the clear sky, then turned obviously adoring eyes toward the orange airhorse.

"It is indeed. But every day we spend with these gorgeous beasts is good."

The big indigo exchanged low, snorted greetings with the charcoal gray airhorse as he passed, but he kept going until he stood beside the orange. The size difference was obvious between them, but so was the affection as they rubbed their strong, arched necks together, snorting and *wuffing* the whole time.

"They like each other," Tonn said again, pretending he wasn't trying to distract Soren so he could get closer to his preferred flight partner. "Landhorses often make lifelong friends when they're yearlings."

Soren's eyes lit up, and he rubbed the broad orange forehead now hanging over his shoulder.

"Do they really? I *always* feel like I'm behind, ever since I got here. There are so few airhorses in Casai, and I didn't get to spend much time around landhorses either." His smile faded, and his face closed off like clouds rolling across the plains. "That didn't exactly help when I tried to explain to my parents why I didn't want to stay there and work as a builder, like the rest of my family. I think they only let me go because they got tired of listening to me."

Tonn's irritation softened, partly because he'd heard the coastal city of Casai was even bigger than Maestar, though he had a hard time believing that. The idea of living an entire life among nothing but endless buildings and streets was even harder to imagine.

He opened his mouth to ask about the constant flow of trading ships docking at Casai, but a great gust of warm, grass-scented breath close against the back of his head stopped him. He turned and found himself inches away from the gray airhorse.

Tonn couldn't help smiling when he saw eyes the same violet as the mane.

"I think *he* likes *you*," Mranes said from behind him. "He's not as big, but he's nearly as agile in flight as this indigo beast."

The indigo airhorse had lowered her head so Mranes could scratch behind her ears, and was now grunting and groaning as she shifted back and forth.

Soren stepped closer and leaned forward.

"I haven't told anyone else, but these two..." He shook his head and smiled again, reaching up to scrub the orange airhorse's neck. "Honestly, they constantly had me feeling like I was about to fall off. A more steady ride like this orange fellow might suit me best, at least until I get more comfortable."

Tonn surprised himself by wanting to offer some kind of reassurance, maybe that Soren would likely improve since he'd started later than most of their base group. But he realized Soren had probably heard more about his older-than-ordinary age than he could stand.

He'd had far more than his fill of his family telling him not to worry, that he'd finally get taller at any minute. The fact that his growth since arriving in Maestar proved them right didn't make the memory of their constant comments any less annoying.

He took in a deep breath, determined to make sure before he shared a word of what was in his mind. The warm scent of the gray airhorse—so like the crackling air right before a huge plains thunderstorm—gave him the comfort and courage he needed.

"That one *is* solid and calm," he said, nodding toward the airhorse now nuzzling Soren's arm and getting a joyful laugh in response. "From the looks of him right now, I'd say he'll be able to fly for hours and hours and never complain once he's grown."

This time when the thundery gray beauty stepped forward, Tonn adjusted his body to accept a remarkably gentle head rub against his chest.

"As for this one," he said, "I expect he'll shoot up to his full growth any time now. Think how strong and quick he'll be then, since he does so wonderfully already."

Tonn somehow knew before he looked that both Mranes and her lovely indigo airhorse would both be watching them, with matching airs of approval. He saw the same expressions and the same small gatherings of yearlings and trainees all over the practice field.

Master Adur, Master Orya, and several others who'd been

working with Tonn's base group stood with their airhorses in front of the green-leafed boundary, their own full-grown and magnificent beasts together off to the side.

All of them watching as the trainees sorted themselves into their own arrangements, riders and airhorses alike.

He turned back to Soren and Mranes and the three airhorses, who he realized were the ones making all the decisions and choices around them. Putting riders and themselves together with no seemingly no effort or argument.

Tonn knew he'd be a very lucky rider indeed with these two as his wingmates. And he couldn't wait to see how he looked in proper riding gear, all violet and stormy gray.

Master Adur was right as she so often was, this time about trusting airhorses and their good judgement.

And their magic.

KARI KILGORE

AUTHOR OF A LINCHPIN LIFE AND THE LAST DRAGONKEEPER

Lines of Strength and Grace

A MISFORTUNE AND MAGIC STORY

For everyone who makes the difficult choice
to leave the past in the past.

ONCE IN A WHILE, when she felt particularly homesick, the newlywed Baroness Dyna Bacalan fought back a strong urge to disrupt the clean, straight lines in her new residence.

The great desert city of Profant boasted a remarkable number of those lines. More than she'd ever imagined possible before she arrived.

Unlike her home along the warm Wrynath Sea—no, not her home anymore, her *childhood* home, near the even larger city of Casai far to the south—the unending orderliness of Profant began with the streets.

She walked along one of them now, surrounded by low conversation and the soft crunching of small brown gravels under the feet of people and a scattering of colorful landhorses, with people and landhorses alike pulling low wooden wagons with boxy white canvas covers.

The gravels emphasized the long, straight lines, cutting through red stone buildings that stretched all the way to towering city walls made of the same squared-off stones.

Dyna tried even harder to ignore her childish desire to kick the clean edges into disorderly rebellion. That sort of behavior was hardly appropriate for a woman who'd not only reached her twenty-first year, but would surely soon become a mother herself.

Or at least she likely could, if she ever decided she was ready.

The buildings and the city walls were all exact lines and perfect right angles, just like the streets. No matter what size the buildings were, from modest houses to cozy merchant establishments to spacious offices for guards or city officials, all the way up to the baronial residence that took up four looming stories and several blocks in the center of the city.

Box upon box upon box, line upon line upon intersecting right angle.

Hardly any windows broke up the solid mass of red

blocks, not with so much heat and dust sneaky and determined to find their way inside. Only thick doors made of pale wood, the grain twisted into fascinating patterns.

With no way for potential customers to peek inside, the merchants all supplied waist-high stalls with colorful awnings in front of their shops to display their wares.

Of course the awnings and stalls were neat and sharp in both construction and contents.

She'd been horrified at the lack of windows at first, coming from a land where openings of all kinds were vital, and carefully positioned to catch the sea breeze at every opportunity.

Then delighted when she stepped into interiors as cool as the caves along the coast, and lit by wonderful metal lamps with bits of colorful glass all around. And perhaps because of all the sharp edges and rigid shapes on the outside, most buildings in Profant held a surprising number of curves and softness within.

Arched doorways and rounded steps, sculpted out of clay made from pale local sand and tinted with beautiful colors. Chairs and tables and even beds made of the same material, with no more right angles than necessary. Luxurious pillows and blankets that would never have done well in the humid seaside air of her youth proved sturdy and long-lasting in the desert.

Even ventilation was handled in a way Dyna hadn't expected. Most rooms in Profant had cleverly hidden grates along the tops and bottoms of the walls, covered with intricately carved stone or metal.

Cool air from vast underground water cisterns was drawn in by the warm air escaping, bringing relief from both heat and dryness.

Only the baron's residence—now hers as well—had windows along interior passages, and throughout the airy healing rooms on the shady side of the house. The healers quite reasonably wanted as much fresh air as they could manage.

Healers who hadn't been able to help Dyna with the first difficulty she'd ever sought them out for. A problem that sent her out into the street on this fine, clear, relatively cool winter afternoon, with the healer she trusted most by her side.

Berga walked confidently in the flowing white garments of her work, keeping her thoughts to herself. Perhaps sensing any attempts at conversation with Dyna would be awkward at best with her current agitation.

Through the jumble of her own fretful thoughts, Dyna had to admit the mass of buildings was impressive, and maintenance had to be relatively easy. Even with Profant's constant wind and frightful sand storms, almost everything looked brand new.

The desert climate could never compete with the fresh sea air of her youth, but the ever-present dust in Profant carried a surprisingly pleasant spicy aroma, almost like cinnamon. She knew parts of the city added more...*challenging* smells, especially around pens and stables for livestock and a broad field outside the city walls where clever pipes carried waste away to dry in the sun.

Thankfully the merchants' row where she and Berga strolled now held only hints of baking bread and roasting meats, stalls full of fragrant herbs and flowers, and a wonderland of perfumes for men and women alike.

She doubted anyone would be likely to get lost anywhere in Profant, even if they wanted to. They simply needed to count the streets as she and Berga both did, and remember when to turn left or right. Or else they'd be faced with the end-point of a towering city wall.

Easy. Clean. Simple.

Repetitive and relentless to her eyes, still tuned to the lush wilderness of the coastlands.

Dyna had grown up in the tiny village of Mychen overlooking the soft Wrynath Sea, all curve and swell, forming itself to the land rather than the other way around. Even though the nearby city of Casai was vast and thriving and busy, it too showed a far more organic design than Profant.

Vast throngs of residents in Casai seemed to understand the labyrinthine streets from birth, and visitors generally knew they'd be better off hiring guides.

Great swarms of children and young adults ran a thriving business escorting crews from countless sailing ships and fishers through Casai's knotted mess of stone, gravel, sand, and even dirt streets.

Dyna couldn't claim to have gained an understanding of those streets, teeming with all manner of people and creatures ordinary and magical. But she'd loved every one of her visits, drinking in all the energy and excitement she could stand and more.

Here in extremely linear Profant, she made a point of returning nods and smiles to everyone she walked past rather than grinning the way she had during city visits as a little girl. Most everyone returned her smile, and many greeted Berga like an old friend.

Dyna wished for such familiarity though she knew it was impossible.

Even hidden by a disguise so simple it proved effective, it would hardly do for the new baroness to leave such a silly, flighty impression by grinning or skipping or laughing the way her younger self had when setting out on any sort of adventure.

Dyna understood the loose, flowing garments everyone wore in Profant, and sometimes she longed for the carefree protection from the brutal heat and sunlight. Cotton robes made of white and other pale colors that covered arms and legs, with light hoods for even more shielding, made perfect sense.

But her new husband had echoed her mother in making it clear such clothing would not be suitable for her outside the privacy of her own bedchamber. She'd do herself—and the barony—nearly as much damage as if she wandered gaily down the streets with her long red hair unbound like an unmarried maiden's.

She was already quite aware of drawing attention to herself with her typical manner of dress, though that truly couldn't be helped when she appeared as baroness beside her husband Hildar.

Today, before she and Berga set off on this secretive journey, Baroness Dyna had worn a closely fitted silk gown more like the fashions of Casai. A rich blue that set off her eyes, with a full skirt cut just above her ankles for ease in walking.

Elbow-length sleeves loose enough to move with her, the front cut low enough for comfort and coolness without risking too much scandal.

Once the wealthier women in the city began copying the style a few weeks ago, Dyna knew she'd exposed just enough of her generous bosom to make an impression rather than offending.

But today she'd switched out the gown for a tan cotton tunic and skirt of her own, and switched her soft slippers for sturdy leather sandals, refusing the risk of painful feet from an ordinary walk.

Between her non-typical clothing and her simply braided hairstyle rather than the elaborate twists and arrangements she usually wore, so far no one had recognized her, out for the first time without her husband or one of the black-clad house guards.

The sense of freedom—and of having a secret—was more

exhilarating than Dyna wanted to admit. What would those wealthy women think of her now?

She rather expected they'd be envious under their disapproval.

Her mother would be *pure* disapproval, and the voice whispering through her head filled in the memory of many scoldings quite nicely.

Despite such shallow and silly musings, right now she wished more than anything that she could count any of the women in Profant as friends, or that she had old friends or sisters or aunties nearby.

Anyone she could turn to with such an odd and delicate concern, and trust to keep her confidence.

Dyna shook her head, dismissing that thought as another of the increasing number of unwanted intrusions from her mother's voice. Berga and the other healers had shown themselves to be nothing but caring and loyal, accepting their new baron's young bride with her strange ways and dubious qualifications as one of their own at once.

Accepting the love between Dyna and Hildar as sincere and true, and holding that as the only qualification needed.

Dyna's own mother had refused to do either.

They approached the seventeenth street from her house, with a stall full of little wooden bins loaded with a wondrous variety of dried grains marking the correct turn on the right. The display, ranging from white to red to bright blue, and from as large as her thumbnail down to not much bigger than grains of sand, matched exactly what Berga described the day before.

"I'm not sure I'm counting correctly," Dyna said, "but isn't the turn just up ahead?"

Berga nodded and flashed her reassuring smile.

"You've counted perfectly, Baroness. I wonder if you've

also noticed the merchant I mentioned as well. I suspect you memorized every word as I described it to you."

"I do pay attention to you, yes," Dyna said. "Though you won't return the courtesy when I ask you to please call me Dyna. Of course I'd tend to pay attention to anyone who's smuggling me through the middle of the city without my husband's knowledge, or approval."

Berga laughed, the clear, musical tone drawing more smiles from passersby.

"This is how I know you're a newly married woman, *Dyna*. You still at least *claim* to believe so many things require your husband's approval. Or that he'd benefit from knowledge of everything you get up to."

"I should think the baron's approval would matter to me as it does to everyone who lives in Profant. Perhaps more so."

This time Berga shook her head and rolled her eyes.

"Our dear Baron Hildar has never been the sort to concern himself with what *everyone* in Profant does, and he'd never get anything else done if he tried. That's why he has guards and spies and officials. And yes, healers. You're part of his system of maintaining order, whether you yet realize it or not."

Dyna scowled as they turned the corner, moving away from the busier main street. On the narrower way, hardly any merchant stands broke the regularity of precisely cut red stone.

She relaxed her face at once, hearing the murmur of her mother's voice in her mind again. Responding to the inner words or disapproving throat-clearing or sniffs often stopped the warning from escalating to knotted shoulders or twisting belly.

"I'm not sure what I could possibly do to help Hildar maintain order," she said. "I barely know my way around my own house, much less this city."

"You'll learn all of that in time, as much as you need to. Don't forget he's almost as new to all of this as you are. He's only held the barony for just over a year. I believe that's a *good* thing myself. The two of you will work out how to help each other as you figure out what you're doing."

Dyna already had her eyes on the house they needed: nine doors away from the cross street. No one else was out, and for the first time she was entirely relieved at the lack of windows.

Hardly any chance of someone recognizing her and reporting back to Hildar, or to anyone else who might care, or disapprove.

She responded to Berga's words without thinking about her own.

"That's one thing my mother kept saying that doesn't make sense. She was certain Hildar wanted nothing more than a pretty young wife he could control. That way he could make sure she fit into his preferred way of doing things and never have to adapt himself."

Berga touched Dyna's shoulder and stopped walking. Her face, tan and lean like almost everyone in Profant, held an impressive scowl Dyna couldn't allow herself without risk of chiding discomfort.

"I may be speaking entirely out of turn, Baroness. But I've known your new husband for many years, since long before I trained to become a healer or he agreed to take on the duties of his title. He may come across as gruff or unconcerned sometimes, and you'll rarely encounter a more stubborn person in Profant, Difeth, or the whole of Hanferthen and beyond. One thing I can tell you is he was *not* looking for a wife to control, nor would he accept one. He certainly wouldn't have traveled as far as your village looking for *you* if that was the case."

Dyna tried to hide it, but she smiled fondly at the memory.

She'd met Hildar in Casai two years ago, when both of them attended the spring trading festival. Joining in with thousands of others celebrating the arrival of the first great ships from across the Nifendraw Sea after the fierce storms of winter.

She remembered the instant their eyes met, how everything inside of her turned to warm liquid at his smile. That still happened when his dark eyes sought her out, and when he smiled at her in a way he never shared with anyone else.

Sadly Dyna's mother never quite accepted either of them as being honest about their feelings or intentions. Dyna suspected that doubt drove her mother's negative response to their courtship and wedding announcement, all the way to the ongoing stream of suspicion and accusation that continued today.

"He certainly made an impression," she said, "arriving without warning like that. I imagine he would have felt foolish if I'd been away when he asked for me. But we'd planned to meet at the next trading festival anyway."

Berga squeezed Dyna's arm.

"All of this is why I wish you wouldn't worry and fret so, Dyna. As long as the two of you build on the care you already have for each other, you'll go forward together."

Dyna stared ahead at the ninth house, otherwise no different from the ones around it. No hint of how her hopes and fears twisted and knotted within both her belly and the nondescript building.

"Everything you just said has me halfway convinced we should turn around and walk away from here, Berga. Forget my silly notions and imagined burdens and go on about my life. My wonderful new life that shouldn't cause me so much tension and distress."

As she had since Dyna first worked up the courage to speak to her several days ago, Berga gave nothing away by her expression or her words.

"We have that option, of course. You're not obligated to go through with this, not even after you walk through the door. I can't make that decision for you. Much like your husband, I wouldn't even if I could."

At moments like this, Dyna wished for a bit *less* understanding and freedom, and more of the clear knowledge of what was expected of her that she'd had growing up. Yes, she'd chafed under that control and all the rules, especially after she met Hildar.

But she'd had fairly easy choices then as well. Do what she should, or accept the consequences of refusing. Which generally resulted in her doing what she should have in the first place. Just with an unpleasant bit of punishment thrown in.

All the while, she got precious little practice in deciding for herself without considering whether rebellion or even protest was worth it.

"Since you brought me here," she said, "you must trust this woman's abilities. So I shall at least hear what she has to say."

Berga lowered her head in the closest thing to a bow she'd offered as they walked.

"As you like. I'll accompany you for introductions, then follow your wishes about whether you'd prefer me to stay or go."

Berga took several steps before Dyna got her own feet moving.

All the courage and determination she'd relied on as she defied her mother's wishes and traveled with Hildar to her new home and new life had evaporated.

Now she only felt uncertainty and a resurgence of home-sickness.

Perhaps if she could smell the sea, or sink her toes into warm sand and water, she'd regain the boldness she needed so badly.

And if she waited—especially if she did return to her mother's house—she'd run the risk of never moving forward in her marriage, or her life.

She stopped beside the door, taking a moment to blot nervous sweat from her brow and above her lips with the sleeve of her tunic. She nodded once.

"I'm ready. Thank you, Berga."

"You may wish to withhold your gratitude, Baroness, until you know how this visit turns out. I hope you find the help you want, and the answers you need."

Like most buildings in Profant, the heavy door had a gleaming metal shape in the middle of the convoluted wood-grain. Decorative as well as functional, and she'd never seen two designs the same.

This one was a perfect brass frog the size of her palm, facing upward with its head leaned back to peer at any arriving guests. Two dusty orange stones glinted where its eyes would be, and another of blood red marked its mouth.

Dyna raised a steady hand without asking, certain she needed to take this step herself. She lifted the narrow hindquarters of the frog, surprised at how warm and heavy it felt as it hinged at the shoulders.

Three quick taps against the brass plate underneath, and she stepped back behind Berga.

Into a position her mother would certainly disapprove of for her baroness daughter, even if she'd been reluctant in her lukewarm blessing of the union. And one Hildar would at least frown over.

But with the metallic knocks still ringing in her ears, she

needed a moment to recover her courage, and to calm the trembling taking over her body.

Before she was ready, the door swung inward, letting out a rush of cool, humid air that her skin welcomed.

The woman standing in the doorway didn't meet one single thing Dyna had imagined.

She stood nearly as tall as Dyna and looked to be in her middle years, but without the lean, almost leathery appearance so many people that age took on after a lifetime in the desert. Her loose cotton dress was a soft lavender that complimented her green eyes and chestnut hair.

Dyna couldn't help returning her welcoming smile.

Berga stepped forward and grasped both of the woman's hands.

"Fami, it's good to see you. I hope you're well."

Fami leaned close enough to rest her cheek against Berga's, then stepped back and let go.

"I'm well any time I see you, Berga." She turned to Dyna and peered at her with a curious expression. "I didn't know who to expect this afternoon, but I must say our new baroness is quite a surprise."

A not altogether unpleasant flush of warmth spread through Dyna's belly at being recognized, along with a motherly hiss of blame and disapproval.

"I hope it's a welcome surprise," she said, holding out a hand. "I'm glad to meet you, Fami. Please call me Dyna, especially since I'm a guest in your home. Thank you for seeing me."

Fami took Dyna's hand in both of hers, as cool as the air inside her house.

"Most welcome, and a lovely break in the routine of my days. Please, both of you, come in out of the sun."

The room inside was simple but comfortable, with several of the colorful lamps hung from the low ceiling and sitting on wooden and earthen tables. The aroma of the refreshing mint and citrus tea everyone in Profant adored drifted through, reminding Dyna how dry her mouth got when she was nervous. A delicate silvery tea service on a plain wooden table explained the enticing scent. Two arched doorways in the same soothing, earthy brown as the walls and ceiling led to other rooms, neither lit well enough to see.

Dyna slipped her sandals off when Berga did, only realizing when her bare feet touched the cool stone floor that she had a scattering of small blisters after all.

A soft and decadent green rug in front of a low sofa formed against one wall offered both luxury and relief. She couldn't help sighing as her tense body sank into darker green cushions that felt like floating on air.

Fami poured tea for all of them into iridescent white cups, handing one to Berga in a nearby chair, then settling onto the sofa beside Dyna. Tiny pink and blue and orange petals floated in the tea, and Dyna breathed deeply before taking a honey-sweetened sip. When she finally exhaled, more of the knots in her back and shoulders relaxed than she expected.

More of the knots than had been relaxed for a long, long time.

"Now, while both of you would be quite welcome for a social visit," Fami said, "please tell me what brings you to my door today."

Before Dyna could work up her courage to speak, Berga reminded her of another question she needed to answer first.

"This is where I must ask you, Baroness, whether you'd like me to remain or give you privacy with Fami. I hope you know I'm glad to support you either way, but the decision is yours."

Forcing herself to ignore the words *your life is none of that woman's concern* shivering through her mind, Dyna instead paid attention to the jolt of fear and loneliness at the thought of Berga leaving.

"I hope you can stay," she said, pretending her voice didn't shake. "I may need... You can help me remember whatever happens, if you're willing."

Berga flashed a half-smile and shook her head, but she sat back in her chair and sipped her tea before answering.

"As I said before, from what I've seen your memory is more than adequate to any demands. Whatever your real reason, I'll wait quietly right here."

Silence went on long enough that it was everything Dyna could to do to keep herself from fidgeting. Then hot shame that didn't feel anything like her own stormed through her chest and heated her face.

"I'm *terribly* sorry, you were waiting for me. Please forgive me." She took another deep inhalation of the fragrant tea, then sipped and let the cooling mint soothe her discomfort. "This is hard to explain, even inside my own mind. But I feel I must try before it drives me mad."

She looked across the room, focusing on one of the cheerful lamps. The flame within flickered a bit from the constant, cleansing flow of air. The effect of tiny rainbows dancing along the wall and curved doorway helped her rediscover her determination.

She spoke without looking away from the colors.

"I've long had a problem with...voices. Not yours or anyone else who truly is in front of me. No, these are unseen, unheard by anyone besides me. I only hear them inside my mind."

"Are there several voices?" Fami said. "Or only one?"

Dyna blinked, surprised by the matter-of-fact tone of the questions. Much like Fami's appearance, it wasn't at all what she'd expected.

"I'm not certain, but I think... I believe they're all

versions of the same voice. I'm afraid I'm hearing my mother."

The last few words took all of Dyna's breath with them, and she held one hand over the thin fabric at her breast. Her heart pounded, leaving her lightheaded.

"Are you truly afraid, Dyna?" Fami said. "Is that why you lost your breath just now?"

Dyna managed to nod, even though the swimmy feeling extended from her head to her chest, then to her arms and legs.

Berga leaned forward, her brow drawn down.

"I don't think this happened when you spoke to me, did it?"

Opening her mouth wide and gasping in air, Dyna shook her head.

"No, not like this. I felt a certain reluctance to speak, and sometimes...sometimes I've had difficulty deciding my own course of action. But now I feel as if I've been swimming too long in the sea, as if I might have trouble getting myself back to shore."

Berga and Fami exchanged a glance, and Fami nodded once before she turned back to Dyna.

"From what you say and your body's reaction, I suspect you have an enchantment. Many of us hear whispers and voices from our pasts, and sometimes those can task us greatly. But the physical distress and your fear tell me you carry something more. Did your mother or anyone else in your family have magic?"

Dyna picked up her teacup with trembling hands and inhaled again before taking a sip. Her heart gradually slowed and she finally drew in a full breath.

"I'm not aware of any of them having magic, but some people in our village did. And plenty of people in Casai either do or claim to. Do *you* have magic, Fami? Have you added something to this tea to calm me?"

Fami raised one eyebrow, but in an amused rather than scolding manner.

"The tea is relaxing primarily because of the flowers and herbs, though I admit the honey comes from a dear friend of mine here in Profant who charms his bees. Yes, I do have magic, but nothing to rise to the level of an Honored Mage. I trained with them when I was younger, but I've gone my own way since, with their blessing. I would never use magic in a case like this unless you ask me to, and only if you understand what you ask."

Dyna bit her lip to keep from blurting out that of course Fami could use magic if it had any chance of restoring control of her own mind. For once she agreed with the heated chorus of *don't you dares* echoing through her mind.

"I'd like to learn more about how we might remove the enchantment before I decide. Is that something you can help me with, or must I seek the help of an Honored Mage?"

"I believe I can help you. If not, I'll make sure we find the person who can. May I ask why you didn't seek out an Honored Mage to begin with? I'm certain one of their number would be more than willing to help the baroness of a city that protects two such important roadways. Some would say the roadways are controlled by Profant, but that's not for me to judge."

"I'm certain mages would be willing to help as well." Dyna stared at her hands, still holding her nearly empty teacup. "I fear word would get back to Hildar if I asked for one, or if I was seen in the company of an Honored Mage he didn't know was here. That's one of the best and worst things about how he thinks about holding the barony of Profant."

She smiled at Berga. "Even if he doesn't overly involve himself in the lives of people who live here, Hildar does prefer to know who passes through our city. Whether they travel from Casai to Dirgelan, Fadlonah to Maestar, or on to another destination, he's aware of the importance of Profant along their path. And he believes his most important role is making sure all operates smoothly."

Fami rose in one graceful motion and refilled all their cups, then resumed her position on the sofa, legs curled underneath her.

"Tell me more of Hildar's role in *your* life, then. Was he considered a suitable match for you?"

Another wave of uncomfortable heat and disorientation passed through Dyna, concentrating in a hot lump in her throat.

As she often had since she announced her engagement to her family and endured their furious response, she reached up and brushed the whisper-fine gold necklace she'd never taken off since Hildar fastened it around her neck earlier that same day. The curved, elongated pendant hung perfectly against the curve of her breasts and held a sparkling blue desert stone the exact color of her eyes.

One that kept its sparkle and fire even in an entirely darkened room.

He'd added a kiss along her hairline that raised delightful ripples across her whole body that had never quite stopped.

A sip of tea dissolved the knot in refreshing coolness.

"No one not chosen by my parents would have been an acceptable match. No lord nor mayor, duke nor baron could have ever had success approaching me before approaching them. My mother would have preferred I never caught sight of my future husband before she had all the arrangements made. Before you ask, because I know *I* would upon hearing this, that's not the typical way where I'm from."

She gently set her teacup down and folded her hands in her lap, determined to keep her discomfort to herself.

"Such formality with courtship and marriage with the firstborn daughter fell out of favor in my mother's family generations ago. To be honest, I suspect she's never forgiven her ancestors for letting the tradition lapse."

Fami didn't reveal anything in her expression, only watched Dyna as she spoke.

"And so your mother revived the practice with you," she said. "Or at least she made the attempt. When did you begin to hear these intensified voices? And experience the physical effect like you did a few minutes ago?"

This time the lump in Dyna's throat seemed to solidify into a hand squeezing tight.

Stealing her ability to speak.

Threatening to block the air itself.

When touching Hildar's stone had no effect, she moved both hands to her neck.

"Are you able to speak?" Fami said softly. She waited for Dyna to shake her head. "Dyna, can you breathe?"

Dyna tried to nod, but the constriction grew tighter.

Fami moved closer to her on the sofa, pulling a string of objects that caught and reflected the light, flashing like the tiny dancing rainbows on the walls. She reached up and touched the back of Dyna's hand.

"I'd like to use magic with you now, Dyna. To relax the hold of the enchantment on your breathing so we can keep talking."

Dyna grasped Fami's cool hand, trying not to hold too tight in her panic. She mouthed "Yes, please," but couldn't even manage a whisper.

Fami pulled Dyna'a hand down and turned it palm up, then placed the flashing objects across her hand. Dyna realized it was a slender chain of silver with gemstones set into it. The stones weren't only catching the lamplight, either. They were glowing with their own internal fire that continued to get brighter and warmer against her skin.

"Take a breath now," Fami said, covering Dyna's hand with her own. "Imagine the air flowing along a wide, open tunnel, pushing aside anything it encounters until there's nothing at all in the way. Look at the strand and let your breath move in the same way."

She moved her hand, and Dyna stared at the gemstones, head pounding as if she'd been holding her breath on purpose.

Now red light moved along the chain, getting brighter in one direction, then the other. Her throat still felt far too tight, but a trickle of air managed to work itself through.

She followed the movement of the light, inhaling slowly until it reached the end, exhaling as it traveled back along the chain's length. Her panic receded as the fluctuating glow shifted from fiery red to orange, then yellow, before it finally faded to a calm shade of muted blue.

And still the brightest point moved along with the rise and fall of her chest.

"Thank you," she said, not looking away from the chain. "What did you do?"

"I only helped you loosen the bonds of the enchantment, much like letting out a garment that's been fit too closely." She blinked and tilted her head to the side. "Or one you've had for many years, perhaps. But now that you're fully grown, it no longer suits you. Do you think you can talk now?"

Dyna slowly breathed in and out two more times.

"I think so. I suppose if I manage to answer your questions, we'll know for certain. I've had that whispering voice as long as I can remember." She paused, then rushed ahead, trying to get the words out before the horrible choking started again. "But it got much worse as soon as I spoke my wedding vows to Hildar."

"Not when you left home or when you arrived here? Only when you spoke your vows?"

"That's right." Dyna's throat felt clear and open, but an iron band seemed to settle into place around her chest. "I was here for three days before our wedding, and aside from not knowing whether it would be worse for my parents to arrive in time or to miss it altogether, I didn't have any special difficulties."

Fami moved away and sat back, her eyes never leaving Dyna's.

"Did they attend your wedding? I'm sorry to say I wasn't able to secure an invitation myself."

Deciding who would be welcomed to the baronial house for the wedding hadn't been part of Dyna's responsibilities that day, beyond inviting her own family. But she still felt her cheeks flush at how many people might have wanted to be there and couldn't.

"They arrived only an hour or so before the ceremony. My parents, my sister, and two brothers. A few cousins and friends were here as well. My mother smiled the whole time, but it..." The constriction around her ribs tightened ever so slowly. "The look of it made me uncomfortable. I would have said it didn't belong on her face, since I don't recall her smiling all that often. But the truth is it may have been the first honest smile I ever saw from her."

The catch grew stronger now, turning her ribs to shards of glass, raising slick nausea in her stomach. Sweat that couldn't possibly make sense in the almost chilly air of Fami's house coated her face and arms and back.

"Look at the strand," Fami said quietly, nodding toward Dyna's open hand.

Dyna scowled at what she saw, and for once she didn't

care about wrinkling her face or what her mother might have to say about it inside her head.

The stones in the middle part of the chain had shifted from blue to a sickly, pulsating green. Dyna was sure the color itself would have made her feel ill if she didn't already. The green was less disturbing toward the ends, but the blue she'd seen when her breathing returned to normal was almost gone.

"Is that showing you what's happening to me?" she managed to force out. "Or are those gemstones causing this pain somehow?"

Berga sat forward, chewing her lip and obviously wishing she could do something to help.

"Those are difficult questions to answer," Fami said. "In your case, it could very well be both. From what you're telling me and what I see in you and the examination through my strand, your enchantment may be reacting to the fact that we're paying attention to it. That seems to be the case when you try to talk about it as well. Does that feel right to you?"

"Does it feel..." Dyna let out a choked laugh and pressed her free hand against her roiling belly. "I didn't expect to talk about my feelings this afternoon."

But the truth was Fami's words *did* feel right, and they matched Dyna's experiences as well. With the deepening pain and sickness in her middle, she didn't much care what happened as long as the torment stopped.

"I don't understand this," she said, unable to stop her voice from rising and her words coming faster even as her breath grew shallow, "but what you say makes sense to me. This horrible cage around my chest keeps getting worse the more we talk. Can we *please* either change our topic of conversation or do something about it?"

Fami leaned forward and covered Dyna's hand again, and her cool touch felt like a lifeline in a dangerous sea.

"Remember what I said earlier, Dyna? About imagining your throat as open and clear? How it eased your discomfort? This is no different. Even with magic involved, your body is in the grips of an illusion your *mind* can control. Lean back with your next breath, expand your chest. Nothing is obstructing your movement, truly."

Dyna squeezed her eyes closed and shook her head, unable to imagine she could break the agonizing hold as easily as that. But the thought of tolerating the tightening vise for even one more second was too much to bear.

She opened her mouth and inhaled, leaning back at the same time, expecting her glass ribs to turn to daggers inside her flesh.

For one horrible second, her worst fear came true, and the crushing pressure threatened to stop her heart as well as her breath.

Then the constriction ebbed away the same way waves on the wide beach did. Leaving ripples and bubbles behind, but taking the bulk of itself back to wherever it had come from.

She wasn't surprised to see the strand still showed a faint hint of green around the middle stones even as the others resumed the healthier, more natural blue. Fami squeezed her hand but didn't let go.

"Did that help loosen the enchantment again?" Dyna said, again blotting at her sweaty face with her sleeve. "Or will it only get worse every time we try to speak of it?"

Fami moved her fingertips to the end of the chain of gemstones, where the blue was strong and solid. Only the one in the center still flickered with unhealthy green.

"The reason I call this an examination strand is it reveals the shape, color, sometimes the motion of a magical construction. I never had enough of the gift of seeing within on my own to become a full Honored Mage, but this gives me a greater level of insight. It also allows me to adjust some constructions, strengthen or weaken or even remove them. From what I can tell, I'm sorry to say I can't remove this one. I'm not sure it *can* be removed, Dyna."

Heart sinking, Dyna raised the hand still holding the silvery strand to touch Hildar's necklace through her tunic.

Then closed her eyes and turned her face away when the small stones flared bright as summertime lightning.

She jerked her hand away and stared down at the swell of her breasts, where her own stone shone right through the gauzy fabric of her tunic, far brighter than it ever had before.

Fami and Berga both lowered their hands where they'd shielded their own eyes.

"May I safely guess that's never happened before?" Berga said, laughing. "I feel you would have mentioned it, and you look as surprised as I feel."

"Never anything like that, no." Dyna pulled the pendant out, distantly noticing the pressure around her chest and throat was entirely gone. "Hildar gave me this when he asked me to marry him. I've worn it ever since."

The stone itself was shaped like an elongated heart, with gold around the edges. Dyna felt an unpleasant chill now that it was away from her skin.

It still glowed brighter than any of the lamps in the room, and the strand of smaller gemstones all matched its blue fire now.

"I wonder if this gift from your beloved activated the enchantment," Fami said, her eyes on the stone. "Or perhaps only agitated it as it set you on the path to independence from your family?"

Dyna started to slip the gold chain over her head so Fami could take a closer look, but Fami held up one hand and shook her head.

"I suggest that gift needs to stay right where it is. How are you feeling now, Dyna? I'll tell you your color is better than when you first arrived, and you're breathing more easily, too."

Dyna glanced at Berga, long enough to see her nodding.

She ran her fingertips along the delicate chain around her neck and touched the lightning blue stone.

"I don't feel nearly as...anxious as before. And you're right, my breath is clear and easy. It's as if Hildar's stone worked with your strand of gemstones to protect me."

"From the way you look when you speak of him," Fami said, "and what I hear spoken all around Profant, it's his love every bit as much as any gift he could have given that protects you."

Dyna closed her fingers around the pendant, surprised at how cool it felt already. The glow was still bright enough to show through her fingers.

"This may sound foolish, or perhaps childish. The stuff of the fairy tales of youth. But I honestly did feel a part of me change when I looked into his eyes for the first time. Like part of me that had been held too tightly relaxed, much like the garment you mentioned. I wonder if... Do you think it's possible my mother sensed that somehow?"

Berga smiled, and her eyes twinkled in the low light.

"I don't know as much of the ways of magic as Fami does, but I do remember seeing three of my older sisters and an older brother through courtship and marriage. In each of their cases, it was our father who knew at once when they brought home the person they would marry. I think he knew before anyone else did."

"If your mother's family *does* carry some sort of magic," Fami said, "even magic old enough to be misunderstood and mostly forgotten, she may have had responded without realizing why. Though I must admit I wonder at that smile of hers you described on your wedding day."

Dyna smiled herself, and it felt like the first honest, relaxed one she'd had *since* her wedding day.

Making a decision she'd been dreading and putting off generally had that effect on her.

"Fami, I would like to work with an Honored Mage to learn more about this enchantment and whether my mother played a role or not. And I'm going to speak to Hildar about this as soon as I get back home. He has his own distrust of magic and mages compared to his own logic and planning and control, but I know he'll support me in this. Is there anything you can do to help until one arrives?"

Fami nodded toward the pendant still in Dyna's hand.

"If you're comfortable with your remarkable jewel being altered a bit more, I believe I can. Has it ever glowed like that, or flashed like fire in the sky?"

Holding the pendant in her palm, Dyna shook her head.

"Nothing like this. It always held its own light. But this has been like turning a single candle into a bonfire."

"Then one more question. Would you be heartbroken if that lovely blue changed sometimes, like the strand you hold does?"

Dyna raised her other hand, where the linked gemstones now cycled slowly through several colors in a pattern she couldn't quite make sense of.

"I think that would be *fascinating*, honestly. Hildar tells me these stones come from deep in the desert, from a place his family knows and protects ferociously. I have other jewelry of the same blue."

Fami moved closer, covering both of Dyna's hands with her own.

"Then what I'd like to do is finish the activation of your stone. It very well may have come from the desert, either here in Difeth or further out into the Harian Desert, where much of the silver used to make magical objects like my examination strand comes from. The contact with my strand was the beginning; that's why we saw such a brilliant flash when they touched. I believe when we're finished, your pendant will have greater protective powers than it does now. And it will likely give you an insight into the state of your body and mind. Are you ready?"

Dyna's breath caught, but not in the painful, constrictive way it had earlier. This was more a thrill of excitement and anticipation.

"I am."

Both Fami and Berga closed their eyes, but Dyna was too curious and happy to do the same. Before she had a chance to wonder how long it would take, a prickly tingle traveled from her hands and up her arms, meeting at her heart and mind before traveling the rest of her body.

The sensation wasn't unpleasant, not exactly. But she wasn't disappointed when it stopped a few seconds later.

When Fami removed her hands, Dyna gasped. Now her pendant rippled through all the colors of the rainbow and more, one after the other. The gems in the silvery strand did the same, and in the same pattern.

"It's beautiful," she whispered. "Do you think it will hold one color later on? When it finishes the activation?"

"I believe it will." Fami picked up her teacup and sat back with a sigh. "I'll be curious how it looks in an hour, a day. Then a week, a month, and more. I do think it will help keep your enchantment at bay. Do you feel more free of it now?"

Dyna slipped her pendant back under her tunic, then gave Fami's strand back and held both of her hands for a second. She took a deep breath, feeling inward for more of those catches and shards of glass.

She hadn't realized how shallow and cautious her

breathing and thinking and the way she moved through the world had become until that moment.

"I *do* feel better. Like my lungs and belly and whole body are filling up now instead of barely sipping enough air to live. More than that..." She placed one hand low on her belly, where she was surprised not to see more of the glowing, expanding light. "Parts of me that were clenched tight are opening now. Making space for whatever comes next."

Berga's nod and soft smile made it clear she understood. Dyna knew in that instant that she'd trust Berga to help with her own passage into motherhood. And the reluctance she'd felt to take that next step in her marriage made sense now.

But a stab of dread cut through the joy aching to grow within her.

"Is this something I'll pass along, even if I don't want to? This enchantment?"

Fami closed both hands over the linked chain of gemstones and sat still and quiet.

"I'd like you to ask the Honored Mage to be sure, but I think it is possible, yes. With that possibility in mind, do you think the baron would be willing to bring these magical stones to your children? If he does, it would be *my* honor to help activate their gifts from their father and help keep them safe."

Dyna's eyes filled with tears. So many things she thought impossible before walking into this house stepped into the world of potential. And even more so at the thought of Hildar making room in his great, warm heart for their children.

"I know he'd be more than willing to do that and much more to protect all of us. Thank you both for making that gift for all of us possible."

All the straight lines and angles of her new home shifted themselves in her mind then.

No matter how they were shaped now, they'd come from the land, from the bedrock underneath the desert. She knew all those sturdy and reliable constructions would help create the strength, freedom, and grace that would sustain her going forward into a bright and unknowable future.

For herself, and for Hildar, and for the family they would create together.

KARI KILGORE

AUTHOR OF ODDS AND ENDINGS AND THE EARWORMS

The Difficulties Ahead

A MISFORTUNE AND MAGIC STORY

For everyone who's admitted a hard truth
and taken the even harder steps to move forward

THE DIFFICULTIES AHEAD

THE FIRE in Lady Selene Sanderlin Knight's private chambers roared much higher and hotter than she normally kept it.

But the howling of a snowstorm outside and the echoes of an equally furious storm inside her heart seemed to call for all that wood and heat and light and more.

The thick stone walls of Castle Knight usually managed to blunt the worst of the seasons, a blessing even if she often needed a much smaller fire for summer evenings. Being able to maintain the comfort of her sanctuary at such a small cost made the occasional draft easy to overlook.

Her tastes ran far less ornate than the sitting, dining, and meeting chambers she'd seen in other nearby castles. Including this one back when her mother-in-law held the title and duty to protect the lands of Fadlonah. Selene had carried out gilt-edged paintings, silver candlesticks and servingware, and enough silk from far across the wild Nifendraw Sea to clothe the entire castle staff in overly delicate luxury.

Now her private rooms—and the bed often shared with her beloved husband Lord Moabar Knight—reflected her preference for sturdy simplicity rather than impressive wealth. Cotton and wool bedclothes. More books than decorations. Simple wooden chairs and a sofa, made comfortable enough for reading those books with the sensible indulgence of plenty of soft cushions.

She kept a ready supply of comfortable skirts and gowns, with elaborate finery reserved only for company who expected it of her.

Selene would have scandalized her own mother with her selection of breeches—far better for a Lady who took every chance she got to tend the colorful Liwith Mountain sheep she'd brought with her. She took every bit as much joy from working in the orchards and gardens around Castle Knight, and tending their stable full of handsome, strong landhorses.

Her pleasure turned to elation on the rare occasion they welcomed visiting airhorses to their number.

Even fourteen years ago, as a newly married woman of not quite twenty, she'd had the good sense to not change a single thing (or take on such firmly untraditional garments and pleasures) while her mother-in-law still held Castle Knight. Selene waited not only until the good Lady Prenema passed the castle and lands to Moabar, but also retired herself south to the much warmer Fynach Coast, before allowing her true preferences and desires to flourish.

Despite her current agitated state, Selene was normally quite diplomatic and able to avoid stirring up unnecessary trouble.

But when it came to her family and especially her children, Selene had no difficulty causing as much trouble as needed to solve the problem.

And she and Moabar had run out of ways to pretend they weren't facing the worst challenge they'd ever had as parents.

She paced restlessly along the thick wool rug in front of the fire, staring as her white-slippered feet passed through each patch of color. From red, to blue, to green, to black, to purple. All the shades of her homeland's sheep brought together in one of her favorite ways to use the leftover bits.

Her other favorite was shared by her sweet son Arch, who was probably snuggled down to sleep under his multicolored wool blanket right that minute.

Selene only wished she could follow him into blissful slumber and forget all the trouble swirling around him like the heavy snowfall outside Castle Knight.

Instead she stalked her own room like some sort of wild spirit, still dressed in her dinner gown rather than holding still long enough to change into her nightclothes. Her midnight-blue tunic and overskirt, chosen to help her feel confident in the face of a challenging discussion, might have backfired.

Now Selene only felt thwarted. Helpless in the realization that she might not be able to help her son at all.

At least not in any way she could yet recognize.

Her long black hair fell unbound almost to her hips, crackling with static in the chamber's dry air. She'd taken up the tradition of leaving it loose only in this room when she married Moabar, longer ago that she wanted to contemplate at the moment.

Even after all those years of marriage and five wonderful children, she blushed to remember how proud she'd been, letting her mother and sisters braid her hair for her wedding day. The first time it had been bound.

A *most* traditional symbol of love and commitment she'd taken on with enthusiasm.

Her family's help that night had come with entirely unneeded advice on how to behave in her wedding bed, more giggly and fun than information Selene would ever want to put into practice.

She paused beside her dressing table at the sound of the

door opening, then picked up a green-tinted goblet. The apple spirit inside was stronger than she usually took in the evening, and cut a path nearly as warm as the fire on the way down.

Even with her beloved husband, she wanted the courage a bit of spirit could lend for this sort of conversation.

She turned as Moabar walked in, and her heart lifted as it nearly always did when she saw him.

His sandy blond hair crackled as well, clinging to the green, hip-length woolen jacket he wore when seeing to the animals with a dreadful storm like this settling in. A bit of silver sparkled in his auburn beard, but otherwise he was as strong and handsome as when Selene first caught sight of him climbing down from the back of a brilliant pink airhorse.

Before she'd ever imagined traveling so far from her Liwith Mountains, much less becoming the lady of such a fine, rich land as Fadlonah.

Moabar brought the scent of wet wool, their always-clean stables, and the brisk snowfall outside. With the mood Selene found herself in, she was thankful he'd managed to brush any snow or mud from his boots before entering into her private space.

He stopped as if he'd walked into a wall made of glass, or perhaps one conjured by the priest who'd recently departed.

After attempting to solve the very problem Selene needed to discuss with him.

"By all the powers that be, Selene, it's fairly roasting in here."

Despite sternly reminding herself to be calm during this conversation all day long, her answer escaped without any sort of moderation.

"Then remove your jacket if you must. These are *my*

chambers, Moabar. You're free to retreat to the chill of your own bed tonight."

He raised his pale eyebrows, but his face showed no other reaction. He did slip out of his jacket and folded it neatly rather than tossing it across the bench at the foot of her bed. The close cut of his black tunic and breeches showed how he'd remained as slender and strong as on their wedding day.

On any other snowbound night, Selene would have spent the last few hours anticipating warming herself in his arms. Not dreading the chill of a rare argument between them.

"Should I ask what the problem is?" he said, sitting in the chair farthest from the fire with his legs crossed. "Or am I correct in thinking you're quite prepared to tell me?"

Selene forced herself to hold still, and to take a deliberately slow and deep breath. No matter how upset she was, she needed to remember he was her ally in this, as he was in so many things.

He was as frustrated and worried about Arch as she.

His fatherly love sometimes showed as a prickly overprotectiveness rather than her own near-desperate desire to solve any difficulty plaguing their children. But Moabar's love was every bit as deep.

"I'm sorry for that, my dearest," she said, lowering her head for a second. "We've had such a rush getting ready for this storm. I hadn't had a chance to truly speak with you since the priest left us two days ago."

Moabar blew out though puffed cheeks, shaking his head.

"I can't say Priest Phellen will be missed. At least not by me. I'm afraid Arch took an even more intense disliking to the man than I did." He stared into the fire for several seconds before turning his blue eyes back to her.

"It shames me to say I've been out and working too much to know this for myself. Have you seen any change in the...difficulties we've experienced here lately? After the priest's visit?"

Selene clasped her hands together to keep from clenching her fists. The fact that she now felt sweat rolling down her back and between her breasts from the overly warm fire did nothing to calm her temper.

But Moabar trying his best to talk around the real problem—and possibly miss the chance at a solution—sent her emotions flaring even hotter.

"What difficulties are those?" She slowly walked over and sat in the chair opposite his. "The unusually early winter storm? The leak that's sprung up yet again in the kitchens? The way Rick keeps outgrowing his breeches before he so much as scuffs the knees?"

Moabar sat forward, clasping his own hands between his knees. Worry etched his features, making him look much older than his thirty-five years.

"No, that's not what I mean. Has anyone had accidents? Or dropped anything? Or have the things themselves ended up broken without anyone touching them at all?"

Selene wished for a bit more of the strong apple spirit, even though it might loosen her tongue more than she wanted.

"As far as I can tell," she said, making an effort to keep her voice calm, "nothing has changed at all on that front. A new young man in the kitchens dropped a pitcher of water at dinner, which promptly soaked Tessa through and through. She reacted about as well as a ten-year-old could be expected to, especially on the coldest night we've had so far this year. One of the serving trays split right down the middle not ten minutes later."

She closed her eyes, trying not to think of how stricken Arch had been when each of those two things happened. How desperately Tessa fought to keep from yelling at him.

The worst had, as usual, saved itself for last.

"And Cogene's son Gahan tripped on nothing at all and landed face-down, on the rug rather than the stone floor, thank all the powers that be. He seems to be developing the knack of landing with an extraordinary amount of grace for an eight-year-old, but that didn't save him knocking his wind out and getting up with a swollen lip."

Moabar rubbed his face, then sat back and stared at the ceiling. Selene knew he hadn't discovered anything fascinating or unusual among the curving gray stones and dark wooden beams, not after living his entire life in this castle. But she refused to prod him to speak, or rush him in any way.

She needed him to join her in understanding what was truly going on, so they could face it together.

"I hope Cogene wasn't terribly distressed," he finally said. "The last thing she needs after losing her husband is something happening to Gahan."

Selene chewed her bottom lip, now struggling harder than Tessa had not to yell.

She was afraid she'd fail where her daughter had succeeded with only a few quickly dashed tears.

She was painfully aware of how Cogene felt about her only child, and how she hurt as much as he did when things like this happened. She'd grown up with Cogene, after all, and knew very well she herself wouldn't have made it through raising her own children without Cogene's help.

Moabar wasn't ten years old, nor was he blind or entirely unobservant. But Selene had long since had enough of pretending the trouble in and around Castle Knight was random, or a simple matter of bad luck.

If either she or Moabar refused to see the truth, nothing would ever improve.

And in truth, Gahan was the only child living in or near

the castle who wasn't already afraid to spend time with Arch. Selene didn't want to imagine the look on her sweet son's face if he lost that last fragile strand of friendship besides his brothers and sisters.

"I'm not nearly as worried about Cogene or Gahan as I am about Arch," she said. "He's the one most affected by all of this. Whatever is going on with him is getting worse, not better. And having this parade of so-called healers gawking at him and spouting such nonsense is making it worse for *him*."

"Then we must put a stop to all of it." Moabar's eyes didn't match his scowl. "He gets his hopes up far too high, and trusts more than he should. Every time *they* fail, he takes that failure upon himself. No more of these fools claiming to want to help with a problem they're creating for their own benefit."

Selene jumped to her feet so quickly the heavy chair shifted over the stones.

She stomped away from her husband, fists clenched tight, then whirled and returned even faster. She stopped so suddenly and close that the full skirt of her gown flared forward around his legs.

He met her gaze, but didn't flinch or say a word.

"They are not *creating* the problem, Moabar! It's not imaginary, and it's not any sort of coincidence. This isn't bad luck that swirls around Arch for no reason at all." Her voice broke and grew ragged, but she couldn't stop now that she was finally putting words to the horrible reality.

"The bad luck is *part* of him. He creates it somehow. He can't help it, and he hates it as much as we do, but none of that changes the fact that he cannot escape it."

He stared up at her, his blue eyes wide and increasingly miserable.

Selene's heart broke for him nearly as much as it did for their son.

"I know what you say is true," he said, his voice rough as well. "But I can't bear to think of it. He's a child, Selene. Just a boy. If I can't hold this dreadful thought in my head, how can we expect him to understand?"

"He understands far too much now. Things can't go on the way they are. He's starting to isolate himself, more than we ever would allow. Aside from Gahan and Cogene, I don't think he's spoken to anyone outside the family for weeks now."

This time it was Moabar's turn to speak harshly.

"Do you think I haven't *noticed* that? I know I'm not around him as much as you are, but I hear what people say. About him. About *us*. About that parade of charlatans. Most don't have the courage to speak to me directly, no. But they have no problem making sure their poisonous words find their way into my ears."

The sight of his fists clenched tight in his lap let Selene relax her own hands.

So often they slipped effortlessly into this dance. Moving forward and back, toward the other and away. Ending up together in the end, no matter how far they each strayed.

But they'd never tried to work their way through anything as awful as this.

She reached out and touched the back of his hand. He sighed and laced his fingers through hers.

"I'm sorry for shouting," he said. "I'm not angry at you, any more than I am at Arch. I've been trying to avoid this whole thing for weeks, to run away from it. That hasn't been fair to either one of you."

"I'm sorry as well." Selene let Moabar pull her forward, and she felt some deep part of her unknot as she settled herself in his lap. "I've been just as long struggling for the words to talk to you about it. Yelling does none of us any good. But I don't know what else to do."

He reached up to stroke her cheek, and she leaned into his touch, resting her head against his shoulder.

"Have you..." he began. "Can you tell whether this difficulty affects everyone? I've seen plenty of other people drop things or break them, trees in the orchard lose limbs, even animals stumble when he's near. But I've never had any of those things happen to me."

Selene shook her head.

"Neither have I. I haven't seen anything happen to our other children, either, not directly. I think Tessa was simply in the wrong place this evening. Maybe family isn't affected?"

"Then at least he might have that much," Moabar said. "People he can spend time around without worrying all the time. Much as I despise the thought of some sort of magical illness or curse or whatever it is, seeing Arch frightened and worried everywhere he goes is much worse."

Selene sat up, running her fingers through his crackling hair.

"Perhaps we should seek the help of an Honored Mage? If this *is* magic, maybe one of them could devise a cure. Or some way to mute the effects."

"I don't know if I could stand to go through this whole charade again," he said, rubbing his forehead. "Or watch Arch go through it. Raising everyone's hopes, then leaving us all in despair. Anyway, in my experience Honored Mages go where they will, and help who they choose. But if the person seems sincere and trustworthy, I won't interfere if the opportunity should ever come his way."

Selene drew breath to suggest they send a messenger to mysterious Dirgelan, the distant city of Honored Mages. Such a message would takes months at best, certainly now that winter had truly tightened its grips on the land. Dirgelan lay far to the north, atop a vast plateau.

Rumor held that the great plateau itself contained the heart of their magic.

Perhaps their landhorse rider would encounter a mage along the way, or an airhorse rider sympathetic enough to help.

Before she could speak, she heard a quiet knock at her bedchamber door.

Moabar's eyes met hers, equally wide and alarmed. No one would disturb them so late without good reason.

She stood and crossed to the door at once, frightened something had happened to one of their children. Terrified Arch's bad luck had affected his family at last, completing his isolation.

Instead of a worried Cogene or an anxious guard, Arch himself stood outside the door. She couldn't remember the last time he'd left his own room after going to sleep.

Black hair so like Selene's standing on end, hazel eyes the same as she saw in her mirror every day, red and swollen. He'd remembered to pull on thick green socks against the freezing cold floor, but he'd left his robe in his bedchamber.

He clutched his multicolored woolen blanket around his little shoulders instead.

Selene knelt and touched his arm, Moabar standing close behind her.

"Arch?" she said. "What's wrong, love?"

His small, clear brow knotted, but he shook his head.

"Come inside, son," Moabar said in a soft voice. "It's plenty warm for all three of us."

Selene reached for Arch's hand, and he stared at it for a few seconds, chin quivering.

Then he let her take his terribly small and cold one, enclosing it entirely in her own.

Moabar put his arm around her as he closed the door,

and he walked the three of them toward a brown sofa a little farther away from the fire.

Once they got themselves arranged with Arch between them—wrapped from his feet to his chin in the wonderfully soft blanket and with a watered-down sip of the apple spirit—Selene resigned herself to the difficult job of waiting.

She knew too well from both her older and younger children that asking a lot of questions right now would only make the conversation worse. And Arch, whether because of his difficulty or because of his sweet nature, was even more sensitive to such parental efforts.

Thank all the powers that be, Moabar remained silent as well.

Arch finally took such a deep breath his shoulders rose, then slowly fell. He spoke clearly for his age, like many children with older siblings, while retaining the high, sweet voice of his youth.

"The man who was here? Priest Phellen? He didn't know how to help me. None of them ever do."

"What kind of help do you think you need?" Selene said, smoothing his hair.

Arch shook his head again, but he when he looked up at her, his mouth was set instead of quivering.

"I don't like making bad things happen to people. I don't *mean* to, but I can't make it stop. The priest and the others want to talk about all kinds of things I can do, or not do. But that never makes any difference."

Selene saw the tension in Moabar's jaw even through his beard.

"Is there anything you think would help?" he said. "Anything we can do?"

Arch leaned his head back, and Selene was struck by the way his pulse beat in his slender neck. He'd probably grow up tall and strong like his father and uncles, but right now, he was so fragile and small.

And she couldn't protect him from the world forever.

She couldn't even protect him inside Castle Knight, inside her bedchamber, tucked close between herself and Moabar.

Not from the invisible thing that hung over him.

"I don't know how to tell people," Arch said, staring at the ceiling like his father had. "That they might get hurt or break things, I mean. They'll be angry at me, or afraid of me. But I don't want them to get hurt. Even if they do decide to stay away from me. I wouldn't blame them if they did."

Selene turned toward the fire so she could blink back tears without him seeing. She'd rather walk out in the driving wind and snow barefoot and dripping wet than add one more whisper of trouble to his mind.

"That's not for you to worry about, Arch," Moabar said. His voice was steady, but when Selene turned back, she saw red around his eyes. "We'll handle talking to people *for* you, understand?"

Arch nodded, not looking away from the ceiling.

"I don't mean to do it," he whispered. "Make all these bad things happen."

Selene touched his soft cheek with the backs of her fingers.

"We know you don't, love. None of this is your fault. Not one bit of it. If anyone *ever* tells you it is, I want you to make sure either your father or I know about it."

She didn't realize how...intense her voice had gotten until Arch sat up and looked at her, eyes as wide as Moabar's had been earlier.

"You really mean that, don't you?"

Moabar met her gaze behind Arch's head, with a half-smile she did her very best to ignore.

At times he was of no help to her whatsoever.

"I do mean it, son, with my entire heart," she said. "We'll figure the whole thing out someday. But don't let anyone torment you or make you feel bad. Promise?"

After a long, somber regard, Arch nodded, with a half-smile far too much like Moabar's to do any of them favors.

"I promise."

He tried to hide a closed-mouth yarn with about as much success as any child ever had.

"Want me to walk you back to your room?" Moabar said. "Tuck you in and make sure you have enough blankets?"

They'd recently moved Arch's bed to the inner chamber of his bedroom, away from the window and the cold stone of the outer wall. Thank all the powers that be, the one unfortunate interaction between him and an unattended fire had been minor, and caught early on.

Arch shook his head with a real smile, and a heart-stopping glimpse of the handsome young man he'd someday become.

Selene firmly refused to think of the possible consequences of his difficulty during those years, which would surely be upon her and Moabar long before they were ready.

"I'm okay to walk myself back. I walked myself here, remember?"

He leaned up and kissed Selene's cheek, and hugged Moabar. Then Arch stood and readjusted his blanket.

Several feet away, the green-tinted goblet that had held his diluted apple spirit tipped over on a perfectly flat, solid table. It somehow didn't break, but the noise was too loud to ignore.

Arch glanced that way, turned to face his parents, and rolled his eyes.

He padded out of Selene's bedchamber without another word or backward glance.

When the door closed quietly behind him, Selene smiled and reached for her husband's hand.

"I suspect he was far more prepared for this than we were," she said.

"I'm afraid he's been living with whatever causes this for longer than we know. Aware of it. But now that we *do* know..."

"We'll do whatever we can to ease the way. Except *stand* in his way. Are you ready for bed, my dearest? I must admit I'm weary."

Moabar raised her fingers to his lips for a kiss, deliberately tickling her with his beard.

"So I'm no longer banished to the chill of my own bed for the night?"

"Not at the moment. I'll inform you at once if the situation changes."

He stood and pulled her up and into a hug.

"Just as you should."

As they walked together toward the bedchamber—and away from the thankfully cooling fire—the knots in Selene's heart loosed themselves a tiny bit.

Their challenges as parents certainly wouldn't be limited to whatever affected Arch.

She allowed herself to hope nothing else turned out quite so strange or surprising.

And to hope they would always manage to support their children and face the difficulties ahead.

Together.

ABOUT KARI

Kari Kilgore's wanderlust and imagination lead her all over the world on grand adventures. Her heart and family bring her home to her native Appalachian Mountains of Virginia. From that solid base, she and her husband Jason A. Adams bring those adventures to life in fiction.

Kari writes fantasy, mystery, romance, science fiction, and contemporary fiction, and she's happiest when she surprises herself. She lives at the end of a long dirt road in the middle of the woods with Jason, various house critters, and wildlife they're better off not knowing more about.

The Confidential Adventure Club

For Kari's exclusive free After The End stories and deleted scenes, discounts, early pre-sale releases, adorable pet photos, and a whole lot more not available anywhere else, join us in The Club.

Hope to see you there!

www.KariKilgore.com
www.SpiralPublishing.net
www.ConfidentialAdventureClub.com

BB bookbub.com/authors/kari-kilgore

a amazon.com/author/karikilgore

g goodreads.com/karikilgore

f facebook.com/kari.kilgore.1

ALSO BY KARI KILGORE

I hope you enjoyed reading the stories in *Fantastic Side Trips* as much as I enjoyed writing them.

You'll find the doorway to the ever-expanding world of Misfortune and Magic at www.KariKilgore.com/MisfortuneAndMagic.

For more fantasy of many kinds, visit www. KariKilgore.com/Fantasy.

Be the first to know about release dates and check out more of my fiction, including almost every genre, at www.KariKilgore.com.

The Storms of Future Past Series:

Dreaming the Storm

Joining the Storm

Into the Storm

Fighting the Storm

Sensing the Storm: A Storms of Future Past Prequel

Storms of the Heart: A Storms of Future Past Romance

Storms of Future Past Books One through Four Collection

The Odd Society:

Independent by Means of Magic

Protected by Means of Magic

The Voices through Time Series:

Songs in the Mountain

Secrets in the Land

Walking the Ghosts: A Voices through Time Novella

Dispatches from the Galaxy Stories:

Restricted Species

The Becalmed

The Garbage Belt

Plurapod Pathogen

The Changes Cascade

Novels:

Until Death

The Dream Thief

Hand Me Downs

Protecting Her Own

Novellas:

Legacy of the Land

In the Pines

DNA Never Lies

The Box of Possibilities

Collections:

Fantastic Women: A Dark Fantasy Novella Trio

Fantastic Shorts: Volume 1

Near Future Forward (with Jason A. Adams)

Fantastic Shorts: Volume 2

Partners in Romance (with Jason A. Adams)

Dispatches from the Galaxy: A Space Opera Novella Trio

Fantastic Shorts: Volume 3

Escape into Romance: A Collection of Sweet Beginnings

Stepping Out of Reality: Short Spells of Appalachian Magic

Facing Down Extraordinary: A Series of Ordinary Heroes

Hacking Cybercrime: Dana Sanderson Short Mysteries

Shadows Mountain Deep (with Jason A. Adams)

Investigations Beyond Belief: The Initial Adventures of Deb Powers: Otherworldly PI

Passages in the Real World: Six Stories of Life's Transitions

ADDITIONAL COPYRIGHT INFORMATION